THE ACCOMPLICE

Norma Charles

RAINCOAST BOOKS

Vancouver

Raincoast Books acknowledges the ongoing support of the Canada Council; the British Columbia Ministry of Small Business, Tourism and Culture through the B.C. Arts Council; and the Government of Canada through the Book Publishing Industry Development Program (BPIDP).

First published in 2001 by

Raincoast Books
9050 Shaughnessy Street
Vancouver, B.C.
V6P 6E5
(604) 323-7100

www.raincoast.com

Edited by Joy Gugeler
Typeset by Bamboo & Silk Design Inc.
Cover design by Les Smith
Cover art by Janet Wilson
Author photo by Brian Wood

1 2 3 4 5 6 7 8 9 10

NATIONAL LIBRARY OF CANADA CATALOGUING IN PUBLICATION DATA
Charles, Norma M.
The accomplice
ISBN 1-55192-430-7
I. Title.
PS8555.H4224A72 2001 jC813'.54 C2001-910179-1
PZ7.C3782Ac 2001

Printed and bound in Canada

For Brian, my life's companion

CONTENTS

ONE

Megan Arnold raced her sister across the kitchen to the phone.

"Megan? Is that you?" Her father's voice floated through the static.

"Dad!" she squealed. Hugging the phone cord, she drew a deep breath. She grinned at Jennifer and gave her a thumbs-up sign. It had been months since they'd heard from him.

Jennifer cupped her pet turtle in her palm and curled up at her sister's feet.

"Dad! Where are you calling from?" Megan said into the receiver. "I can hardly hear you."

There was a pause, then her father's voice again. She strained to make out what he was saying. At the table, her mother had stopped polishing the silverware to listen.

"I'm calling from the fish farm," he said. "I finally got their cell phone to work. It's great to hear your voice, Meg."

"You too, Dad," she said, jumping on one foot and winding the cord around her arm.

"I'm planning to be in town this long weekend and I was hoping to see you and Jen," he went on. "Maybe we could even spend the holiday together."

"That would be so terrific!"

"I could bring you out to the island I was telling you about. I've got a surprise there I can't wait to show you."

"A surprise!"

"You haven't mentioned the island to your mother, have you?"

"No, no. Of course not. You told me not to." Megan lowered her voice and turned away from her mother.

"Good, good ..."

"Who did you say you were speaking to, Megan?" her mother asked.

"It's Dad! He's coming into town and he wants Jen and me to spend the whole weekend with him!"

"What? But you can't this weekend. It's Thanksgiving and, except for a meeting on Monday, I have the weekend off for a change. I kept it clear especially so I could spend time with you two. And we have reserved tickets for *Les Mis* on Saturday night. Have you forgotten? Here. Give me that." Megan's mother snapped off her rubber gloves and reached for the phone.

"But, Mom ..." Megan said as her mother scooped the receiver out of her hand. She spun away angrily and glared at the back of her mother's head.

"Joseph," said her mother into the phone.

Silence.

"Yes, it's me," she said, her voice cold and hard as cement. "No, you can't have the girls on the weekend. We've made other plans. You can't show up out of the blue and just snap your fingers and expect everyone to jump. You know it doesn't work like that."

Silence.

"No, Joseph," she went on, drumming her long fingernails on the wall beside the phone. "The answer is no. N. O. You haven't bothered to see the girls for the better part of a year. You didn't even call on Megan's birthday. She was heartbroken."

Megan shook her head in protest. Why did she have to tell him *that*?

"Okay, you go right ahead. You call your lawyer." Her mother's voice rose. She was almost shouting now. "That's fine with me. But the girls and I have other plans. And they don't include you!"

She hung up with a loud clatter and sighed heavily, exasperated. Her cheeks were flushed and her eyes shone with anger.

"You can't do that, Mom! You can't just hang up on him. We don't know his phone number. We can't even call him back!"

"Oh, that man! He hasn't changed a bit. He thinks he can just waltz in and make demands and everyone will bow to his wishes."

"But I *want* to see him. *We* want to. Right, Jen?"

Jennifer was still sitting on the floor, stroking her pet turtle. She looked up at Megan, confused, but she blinked hard and nodded.

"There'll be other times, girls," said their mother through stiff lips. "As I told him, we already have plans for the weekend."

"But I don't want to go to that stupid musical," wailed Megan. "We haven't seen him for months!"

"I've already bought the tickets," said her mother. "Do you know how much I had to pay for them?" She tugged her rubber gloves back on and started polishing the silverware with renewed vigour.

"Why do you have to be so mean? You won't even let us see our own father! If it weren't for you, he'd still be here, living with us. You're ruining my life!"

"It's not like that, Meg. Really it isn't. Your father can see you any time he wants, but he has to give us some warning first. That's only fair. He can't just show up whenever he wants to and expect …"

"But he's our *father*! He has rights too. Now he'll probably never call us. Maybe we'll never ever see him again."

"I'm sure he'll call again and I'm sure we can make arrangements for a visit some other time. Come on now, finish loading the dishwasher. Then we'll have a piece of that nice frozen chocolate cake for dessert. How about that?"

Megan stomped back to the dishwasher. She ground her teeth and shoved in the supper dishes. Her mother's favourite coffee cup, the one that had SUPER

MOM printed in red on the side, slipped from her hands and fell. It smashed into a hundred pieces.

"Oh, Meg ..." Her mother arched her eyebrows at her.

Megan stormed out of the kitchen and up to her room. She kicked everything out of the way and flung herself onto the bed, her insides twisting into a tight tangle. Why did her mother have to be so unfair?

She hated every single thing about her, she decided. She hated the way she arched her thin eyebrows whenever Megan did something she didn't like. She hated her frizzy blond hair which she had to have streaked every other week at the hairdresser's. She hated her long red fingernails and fancy clothes. She hated how she was always too busy working to spend time with her and Jennifer.

She hated the way she was changing their house, charging through each room like a cyclone, throwing out the old and dragging in the new. Just because she was an interior designer, didn't mean she had to practise at home. What did she think it was? A fancy display home from *Better Homes and Gardens*?

She hated the cold, shiny black kitchen floor and black chairs. Even their new fridge was black. Black, black, black. Everywhere you looked in that grim kitchen was black. And her mother thought it was *sooo* sophisticated. Why couldn't they be an ordinary family and live in an ordinary house like other kids?

And now *this*. All because of *her*, she would miss seeing her dad completely. How did she end up with a mother that was so mean?

She clutched her stomach and moaned, rocking herself back and forth. Tears streamed down her cheeks. She sniffed hard and pounded her pillow with her fist. Then she picked it up and, with all her might, she hurled it across the room.

Megan and Jennifer were out on the back deck after school the next day. Megan was doing some warm-up exercises before shooting baskets at the hoop attached to the garage. Her friends, Sandip and Lucy, often came over to join her, but today she felt like being alone. Mrs. Milton, a grandmotherly woman from down the street, used to look after her and Jennifer until their mother came home from work, but now that Megan was twelve and old enough to baby-sit, she usually looked after Jennifer herself.

The telephone rang.

Megan ignored it. She was doing the leg stretches her new gym teacher had shown the class.

"Aren't you going to answer that?" Jennifer said, nudging Megan's shoulder with her knee. She was sitting on a deck chair and feeding her turtles their daily dose of chopped lettuce.

"Why don't you?" grunted Megan, imagining her leg muscles stretching out like thin rubber bands.

"I'm feeding Tweedledee and Tweedledum their after school snack," said Jennifer. "Turtles get hungry, you know."

The telephone kept on ringing.

"On the other hand, maybe it's Sandip calling about our Science homework assignment," said Megan. She rushed through the kitchen to answer the phone and bashed her elbow on her mother's glass table. The black lacquered vase of artificial flowers in the centre tumbled over and crashed to the floor. Stupid table. Ugly flowers. She clutched her throbbing elbow and grabbed the phone.

"Megan? Is that you?" her father's voice crackled through the static.

She felt her face break into a wide grin. "Dad! It's you!"

There was a pause, then, "So how are you doing, my Meg-Peg?"

"Okay. Are you calling from that fish farm again? I can hardly hear you."

Another pause, then his voice came through the static again. "Yes. The fish farm. We were kind of cut off yesterday."

"Right. I don't know why Mom got so upset. She didn't let me get back on the phone. I'm sorry she hung up on you."

"Is she home from work yet?"

"No. She doesn't usually get home until after five. Jen and me, we're on our own." She stared out the window at the dusty rocks in her mother's fancy new Japanese garden beside the driveway.

"I'm still hoping to come to town tomorrow and I'd sure love to see you."

"Really? Even after what Mom said?"

"Sure. I could meet you somewhere."

"You mean, um, not even come to the house?"

"I think it would be better if I picked you up some place nearby. You name it."

"Without Mom knowing?" Her scalp prickled. A shiver of uneasiness trickled down her spine.

"Right. Would you do that for your old papa?"

"I don't know, Dad ..." Her mind reeled. What should she do? If she did sneak out to meet her father, her mother would be furious and she'd get into big trouble. She picked at the fallen flower arrangement and crushed a black petal between her thumb and forefinger. It smelled dry and faintly musty.

"I could meet you on Tenth Avenue and we could go out for lunch or something," he persisted.

"Sure. I guess." She thought for a moment and took a deep breath. "How about in front of the library?"

"Sounds good to me. Maybe you could come out here to that island I was telling you about and I could show you my surprise."

"Out to your island?" Megan's voice squeaked. She realized her hands were sweaty so she wiped them on her shorts and rubbed the back of her neck. She raked her fingers through her hair and tucked it behind one ear.

"You haven't told your mom about my island, have you?"

"No. I told you yesterday. You said not to mention it so I haven't." She glanced out the window again. Good. No sign of her mother's red Celica. She narrowed her eyes and remembered how furious she was at her anyway.

She also remembered her mother saying she shouldn't tuck her hair behind her ears; it made them stick out and look enormous. She flicked her hair out again and smoothed it down.

"Good. Good," her father was saying. "We don't have to worry about her then."

She cupped the phone and lowered her voice. "I'd love to see you, Dad. But what about Jen?"

For a second she hoped he would say, "Come alone, Meg. I want to see just you." She'd finally have her father to herself for a while. At the moment she couldn't think of anything better.

Instead he said, "You could tell her you need some books for your homework from the library and ask her if she wants to come along. Is she still crazy about dinosaur books?"

"Sure. She gets a new stack every week. Don't worry. She'll come. I'll think of something."

But she knew it would have to be something more exciting than an ordinary library visit to pry Jennifer away from her Saturday morning cartoons.

"And, Meg. You won't say anything to your mother, will you? You know how she can worry. I don't know what was the matter with her yesterday, saying I can't see you. Can you believe it? You're still *my* children and besides, time is precious. I want to see you *now*, before you're all grown up."

"Okay. Um, I guess." What else could she say? After

all, he *was* her father. She perched on the edge of the chair and wrapped her feet around its legs. The black lacquer felt clammy against her bare calves. "What time should we be there?"

"How about eleven? That should give us enough time to grab some lunch somewhere."

"Okay. See you at eleven in front of the library. You can count on me."

"Who's that on the phone, Meg?" asked Jennifer, heading for the refrigerator to get more lettuce.

"The phone?" said Megan, clumping down the receiver. "Oh, that was ... Lucy. You know, Lucy Falls."

"I thought you weren't friends with her anymore. Ever since she ..."

"Oh, she's not all that bad, I guess." Megan cleared her throat. She couldn't stop herself from grinning, she was so excited. "Hey, how about good old fish and chips for supper?" She skipped over to the refrigerator.

"We have fish and chips every Friday night. Let's have pizza for a change."

Megan opened the freezer. It was full of packages her mother had labelled and organized into neat piles.

"You're in luck. One package of Hawaiian pizza left. I'll put on some extra cheese and green peppers and stuff."

"No mushy mushrooms on mine."

"Okay, okay. Hey, tomorrow morning ...?" Megan began just as high heels tip-tapped across the front porch.

A key turned in the lock.

"That's Mom! Never mind. Tell you later." Megan pressed her lips together and ripped open the package with more than usual force and dumped the frozen pizza onto a baking sheet.

Her mother called from the front hall, "Hello? Oh, there you are!" She came into the kitchen trailing her briefcase. "Starting supper already? That's great because I'm starving. My new diet doesn't allow any snacks between meals." She kicked off her high heels and opened her arms wide for a hug, but Megan bristled and pulled away.

Jennifer burrowed her blond head into her mother's shoulder.

"Hi, Jen. How's my sweetie-pie?"

Megan picked up the paring knife and slashed open the cheese package. She might never hug her mother again. Ever.

Her mother gazed over Jennifer's curly hair and smiled at Megan, the corners of her mouth curving upward, but Megan just narrowed her eyes and frowned. She concentrated on hacking up the cheese into a thousand tiny bits.

TWO

"Can't you ever sit still, Meg?" complained Jennifer that night. "You're driving me crazy! Do you have to bounce your ball in front of the TV like that? Look! You made Tweedledum fall off his pillow again."

"Your stupid turtle shouldn't be on the couch anyway." Megan pressed the channel changer and the TV flicked to the basketball game.

"Hey! I wanted to watch the rest of *Couch Potatoes,*" yelled Jennifer.

"You're so busy with those dumb turtles, you're not even watching it. I bet you've seen that episode a dozen times already anyway. Besides, it was just a commercial." Megan rolled her basketball from foot to foot. "Look! Vancouver's winning, 32-20!"

"Watch out! You almost squashed Tweedledee with

your ball!" squealed Jennifer.

"Holy tamales! Put those turtles back in their box where they belong. They shouldn't be crawling around all over the place like that."

"They need their exercise." Jennifer gently pushed her turtle to encourage him to move forward. "Everyone needs exercise, you know."

"Speaking of exercise. Tomorrow morning ..." Megan started. But she still couldn't think of how to get Jennifer to skip cartoons and go to the library to meet their father. Besides, their mom was in her study right next door and could hear every word.

"What about tomorrow morning?" asked Jennifer.

"Oh, nothing," said Megan. Her favourite player, Nat Tucker, had the ball. He was dribbling it down the court. He was in the clear. He was taking the shot ...

The TV picture flicked to Bart Potato's face.

"What's the big idea?" Megan shouted. "I'm watching the basketball game!"

"But I'm watching my show and I was watching first."

"Give me back that channel changer!" Megan grabbed it. Jennifer jumped on her and they started wrestling on the floor.

"Watch out! You'll squish Tweedledum!" shrieked Jennifer.

"Girls!" shouted their mother from the next room. "For heaven's sake! I've had enough of your bickering." She appeared at the door and stared at them over her reading glasses. "I won't stand for this another minute."

"But I want to watch the basketball game," said

Megan. "Vancouver's winning for a change."

"But I started watching *Couch Potatoes* first," whined Jennifer.

"Megan. You know the rules. If Jennifer was watching a program first, let her see the end of it."

"You always stick up for her. Besides, she wasn't even really watching. She's too busy with those stupid turtles."

"I am not."

"Are so."

"If you two can't get along, the TV is going off right this minute," said their mother, flicking off the set. "And you can both go straight to your rooms."

"That's not fair!" said Megan. " I *never* get to watch a whole basketball game."

"No more TV tonight for either of you," said their mother. "I have to get the Moodie's report done so I can have the weekend off. Now, up you go, both of you. I need a bit of peace and quiet."

Megan grabbed her basketball and thumped upstairs to her room. Maybe she wouldn't bother telling Jennifer about meeting their father tomorrow morning after all. Then she'd miss him. Too bad for her. It would serve her right.

That night Megan stared at the face of her clock radio: 11:06. She couldn't sleep. She couldn't even close her eyes. Tomorrow. Tomorrow. How many more hours? In less than twelve hours she was going to see him. She couldn't wait. She wrapped her arms tighter around herself.

It was too hot under her heavy blankets. She tossed back and forth. She kicked off the covers and stared at the clock radio again. She knew that she wouldn't be able to sleep for a single second the whole night.

What if her father had completely changed since the last time she'd seen him? When was that? It must have been at least six months ago. No, longer. It was sometime last fall so it must have been almost a year. It felt like three lifetimes ago. They hadn't even seen him at Christmas because he had to be out of town on business with his chartered accountancy firm. What if she didn't even recognize him? Maybe he wouldn't recognize her!

She stared down at her feet and wiggled her toes. Her feet had sprouted about five centimetres overnight and most of her clothes were way too small, too tight and too short. She couldn't stop herself from growing. Sometimes she tried to eat less but she was always so hungry. Here she was, twelve years old and in grade seven, the last grade at Queen Mary Elementary School, and she was one of the tallest girls in her class. Not that her height helped her all that much; she was still a lousy basketball player.

She reached down beside her bed and rolled her basketball closer. Then she sat up and cradled it in her arms, feeling its rough, dimpled surface with her chin and inhaling its rubbery smell.

Basketball was one thing she and her father had

always had in common. They'd watch most of the games on TV together and for her birthday four years ago, he had given her a regulation-size basketball and a hoop. Her mother had said that it was a ridiculous present for an eight-year-old girl. She had given her a jewellery-making set that Megan had stashed at the bottom of her closet and never even opened.

That year, her father had attached the basketball hoop to the garage and taught Megan how to dribble in the driveway. She and her friends used to spend hours out there, practising various moves and shooting baskets before a game: three of them against her father.

"You have to concentrate," he would tell them. "You have to visualize the ball swishing through that net."

But shortly before her tenth birthday, he developed a new interest: long distance cycling. He had usually cycled to work before, but after joining a cycling club, he began to take longer trips. Sometimes when he returned, he'd be so exhausted he'd flake out in front of the TV, with a couple of beer or a tall glass of rum and coke, and fall asleep. He couldn't even stay awake for the NBA finals. Megan had to watch them alone.

She hugged her ball close and curled up under the covers again.

To please him, she had begged for a mountain bike for her birthday. But it was too late. He'd lost interest and soon after her birthday party, he moved out to live in an apartment downtown. At first she and Jennifer went to visit him there on weekends, but for the past year or so, except for an occasional phone call, they had lost contact with him. She wondered if he still lived in the same place.

When she finally fell asleep, she had a dream. In the dream she was on her mountain bike, flying down a street lined with cherry blossoms. She dreamt she was climbing one of the trees with her father, drifting among the sweet-smelling blossoms. They glided from branch to branch like two graceful monkeys. As they swung, delicate white flowers swirled around them like a fragrant cloud of confetti.

But the white blossoms soon drooped and withered into black lacquered stalks. She crushed them between her fingers and they smelled dry and faintly musty.

She woke with a start and stared at her clock. Nine-thirty already! How could she have slept in? And she still hadn't figured out a plan to get Jennifer to the library to meet their father. Maybe she wouldn't bother. She'd leave Jennifer behind. But she knew her father wouldn't go for that. He'd specifically asked her to bring Jennifer along and she had promised him she would. A promise was a promise.

As she tugged on her beige shorts and a black T-shirt with CONVERSE BASKETBALL across the front, she heard the drone of the TV in the den just below her bedroom. Good. Jennifer was already up. She broke open a new package of black sports socks, pulled on a pair and headed downstairs.

She stood in the doorway of the den and looked at

Jennifer sprawled out on the carpet in front of the TV, mesmerized as usual.

She shook her head. Those fuzzy pink pajamas Jennifer was wearing were for babies, not for an almost eight-year-old. She had outgrown them long ago. When the toes had worn through, she had hacked off the feet, and now the pajama legs ended at her knees. Still, she insisted on wearing them to bed every night, except when they had to go into the laundry.

In fact, most of Jennifer's clothes were too small and babyish. She wore new things only when their mother insisted. It was as if she didn't want anything to change, as if she were trying to keep things the way they had been a couple of years ago, in the days before their father had left them.

But that wasn't the problem at the moment. How was Megan going to get her to Tenth Avenue by eleven o'clock to meet their father without Mom knowing?

"Jen," she began. She scratched the sole of her foot against her leg, thinking. "Um, Jen. There's a special program on at the library this morning. Want to come with me?" she tried.

Jennifer ignored her and stared at *Dino Babies*.

Megan had to stand right in front of the TV to get her attention.

"Hey! Get out of the way! I'm telling ..."

"Just listen to me a sec, Jen. You have to ..."

Mom popped into the den. Her tousled blond hair bounced. She was still wearing her silky white dressing gown.

"You two aren't still arguing about TV, are you? How about some yummy pancakes and maple syrup for brekkie this morning to start off our Thanksgiving weekend? I'm starved."

"No. We can't," said Megan. "We don't have time." She knew her mother could spend the whole morning concocting a complicated breakfast like *Crêpes Suzette*.

"No time? What are you talking about? It's Saturday. Not even ten o'clock yet."

"There's this, um, this program on at the library on Tenth," Megan lied. "About dinosaurs. I was just trying to tell Jen about it. Starts at eleven. We can't be late."

"About dinosaurs? I didn't see anything on the events board when Jen and I were there last Saturday."

"They announced it at school yesterday," Megan said quickly. "And since our next unit in science is going to be on prehistoric life, our teacher said we should all check it out." She was thinking fast. Funny how the soles of her feet became unbearably itchy when she was nervous, or when she was lying. She rubbed her foot on the rough carpet.

"Dinosaurs?" Jennifer actually unglued her eyes from the TV screen. "Did you say dinosaurs?"

Megan knew it. Dinosaurs always worked.

"Right. Eleven o'clock at the library. And everyone's going, so there's bound to be a lineup. That means we have to leave early to get a good seat. First come, first served." Megan tried shoving her itchy foot into her basketball shoe, but the itch was driving her crazy so she had to take off her sock and give her foot another good scratch.

"Just a minute," said their mother. "You girls aren't going anywhere without breakfast. Breakfast is the most important meal of the day. Have a bowl of cereal at least."

"Okay. But no pancakes."

A few minutes later, the three of them were sitting at the kitchen table. While Megan gulped down her cereal, her eyes remained fixed on the kitchen clock: 10:20. Gulp, gulp. Amazing how your throat would not cooperate when you had to eat fast.

Her mother sat across from them, her hands around her cup of black coffee.

Megan looked through the glass tabletop at her own feet tapping nervously against the chair leg. She pressed them together to stop.

Her mother stirred Sweet 'n Low into her coffee. "Wonder what I should do this morning? Except for e-mailing that report to the Moodies, I'm totally free. No open houses or home shows to worry about for a change. I told them at the office that I didn't want to be disturbed so I could have this whole weekend off to spend with you two."

"Right, right," mumbled Megan, spooning cereal into her mouth at a rapid pace.

Her mother shook her head and flipped though the morning paper.

"Oh ho!" she said. "A sale at Sardine's on Tenth. I'll check it out if you're going to be busy all morning."

"Sardine's!" Megan choked. Sardine's Ladies Wear was practically next door to the library! She cleared her throat and said, "Sardine's has such frumpy clothes, Mom. You don't want to go there. They'd make you look like an old lady."

"Do you think so?"

"Their clothes are just for old, old ladies, like my teacher. Frumpy old teacher clothes. I bet she shops there all the time." Megan's legs were swinging like mad. She stopped abruptly and forced herself to be still. "I heard they're having a big sidewalk sale at Oakridge mall though. You should check that out. Maybe Jen and I could meet you there for lunch later and I could get some new jeans. And Jen could sure use some decent pajamas."

"Could not," said Jennifer. She sat beside Megan, feeding a Cheerio to one of her turtles. She had changed into her favourite weekend outfit, a tatty pair of pink shorts and a matching T-shirt with baby turtles on the front. She had to keep tugging the shirt down to cover her round stomach.

"Maybe I could get you a new leotard for ballet," said their mother. "I noticed last week at your lesson that your old one was getting a bit tight."

"Don't you know that you shouldn't feed animals at the table?" Megan told Jennifer. "It's very unsanitary."

Jennifer screwed up her eyes at her sister and continued to feed her turtle.

"Meeting for lunch at the mall is a great idea," said their mother. "You could take the bus from the library, so don't forget your bus passes. Maybe we could even find something special for you two to wear to *Les Mis* tonight."

"*Les Mis*?" said Megan. "Oh, right, the musical." She gulped and stared down at her hands. She couldn't meet her mother's eyes.

"I know you'll love it," her mother went on. "It's had terrific reviews. They said the choreography is really something. Anyway I could wait for you two at the Food Fair, in front of that pizza place. Think you'll be finished by one o'clock?"

"Should be. I'll just get my notebook." Megan zipped up to her bedroom and grabbed it from her desk. She ripped out a blank page and scribbled a quick note: *We're with Dad so don't worry about us. See you soon. –M.* She hesitated and bit her lower lip. Should she really be doing this?

Her father would soon be there in front of the library, waiting for them. Maybe he was there already!

She quickly folded the note and looked around the room. Where could she leave it so her mother would find it, but not too soon? On her bed. She wrote MOM on it in block letters and propped it up on her pillow before rushing back down the stairs.

"Come on, Jen. We've got to get going." She grabbed their bus passes from the black box on the counter and tugged at her sister. "Are you coming, or not?"

"I'm coming. I'm coming." Jennifer gently placed her turtle back into its box. "In you go, Tweedledum," she murmured. She put the lid down gently, picked up the box and followed Megan to the door.

"Where do you think you're taking that?" Megan asked.

"They want to go to the dinosaur show too," Jennifer said. "After all, dinosaurs are one of turtles' closest relatives."

"Holy tamales! You're impossible! Here. Grab your jacket. We have to get going. Now!" She tossed Jen's coat over her head.

"I don't need a jacket. Look, it's sunny out."

"Better take it. You never know."

"Bye, Mom."

"Bye, sweethearts. See you around one." She flicked the newspaper to the HOME section.

"Don't worry if ..." Megan started. Her mother looked up, her eyes questioning. "If, you know, we're a bit late, or something."

"I'll just have a coffee and wait for you," said her mother, smiling.

Megan's last glimpse of her mother was of her sitting at her glass-topped table, steam rising from her coffee cup as she flipped though the morning paper with her long red fingernails.

Megan felt a twinge of guilt, but she *had* left the note so her mother would know that they were with their father. She just hoped that she wouldn't find the note too soon and come running after them before they even had a chance to talk to him.

She marched down the sidewalk away from the house, head down, her long basketball high-tops slapping quickly against the cement sidewalk. Slap, slap, slap.

"Wait up, Meg," puffed Jennifer. "I can't keep up. What's the big rush?"

They were more than a full block away now. Megan glanced back. Their mother had not come after them. Maybe it was stupid to have left the note. But on the other hand, she knew that her mom would be out of her head with worry when she and Jennifer didn't show up at the mall this afternoon.

"Listen, Jen," she said. "I've got something to tell you. There's really no dinosaur show at the library this morning."

"I knew it!" Jennifer stopped abruptly. "Well, I'm going home. I still have time to watch *Star Girl*." Her runners squealed on the sidewalk as she whirled around.

"No, Jen. Wait!" Megan lunged after her and grabbed her sleeve. "It's something even better. Tons better."

"What? Nothing could be better than a dinosaur show."

Megan took a deep breath and let her have it. "We're going to meet Dad!"

"Dad!" Jennifer's face broke into a grin. "Really, Meg? You're not just saying that, are you?"

"Really, really! At eleven o'clock in front of the library."

"Why didn't you say so? And why didn't you tell Mom?"

"Of course I didn't tell her. I couldn't. She'd never let us go. Didn't you hear her telling Dad on the phone that he couldn't see us unless he gave her some warning? But he phoned again yesterday and said he would meet us at the library this morning. Not only that …"

She stopped.

"Not only what?"

"Never mind. Let's hurry. We can't be late. He's probably waiting for us right now!"

THREE

But their father wasn't waiting. The girls stood in front of the library entrance and watched people come out with backpacks full of books.

"Think I have time to check out that new *Dinosaur Encyclopedia* before Dad gets here?" asked Jennifer.

"No," said Megan. "He'd probably come the minute we went inside and then we'd miss him."

Next door to the library was a bakery. The scent of fresh baked bread drifted through its doors. Megan's stomach grumbled with hunger.

"You got any money?" Jennifer asked her, eyeing the jelly donuts in the window.

Megan's hands explored the pockets of her shorts: a button from her jacket and the bus passes. She shook her head. "Wish I did. Oh, no! There's that nosy Mrs. Persky and her dog!"

"Hello, girls," their neighbour said in her shrill voice. "I'm *so* glad you two are here. What luck! They won't let Lana into the bakery, so could you keep an eye on her for me? I won't be but a minute."

Before Megan could object, Mrs. Persky had dropped the dog's leash into her hand and disappeared into the store.

The dog was particularly ugly, with quivering pink skin and black and white speckled hair; and there was a silly purple ribbon stuck between her ears. She sniffed around Megan's knees with her damp nose and left slobbery wet streaks on her bare legs.

"Now what?" she said to Jennifer. "When pesky Persky comes out she'll ask us a pile of questions. Come on."

"We can't just leave Lana here," said Jennifer. "What if she runs out into the traffic?"

"We can tie her leash up to the railing and hide in Sardine's. With that sale crowd, they probably won't even notice us." She quickly wrapped the dog's leash around the railing. "Okay. Let's split," she hissed at Jennifer. "Hurry, before Persky comes out."

As they slunk past the bakery window, the dog started to bark frantically. Before they could escape into Sardine's Ladies Wear, the barks had become howls, loud, lonely howls.

Mrs. Persky rushed out of the bakery. "Oh, my poor, poor baby!" she cried. "What have those bad girls done to you now? Where have they gone?"

Megan shoved Jennifer into the crowded store and

they ducked behind a dress rack. A saleswoman was watching them so Megan started ruffling through the dresses. What she had told her mother was definitely true. These dresses were frumpy.

"May I help you?" the saleswoman asked, eyeing her suspiciously.

"No," said Megan, shaking her head sadly. "Not really my style."

As she and Jennifer meandered back to the door, Megan saw a rack of colourful silk scarves. She stopped to examine them, but she didn't dare stay too long. For one thing, that saleswoman was still staring at them. For another, their father might be outside looking for them. What if they missed him? But how could they sneak past Mrs. Persky?

Megan noticed a small green car parking at the end of the block, shunting back and forth into a tight space.

A man came out and examined the car as if inspecting it for damage. He had a thick, dark moustache and beard, but there was something familiar about him. He was tall, had long dark hair and square shoulders, and was wearing a felt hat with a floppy brim. Her stomach lurched.

"There he is!" she squealed. She grabbed Jennifer's sleeve. "He's here!"

She tugged Jennifer outside and they both sprinted to the corner, calling, "Dad! Dad!"

He leaped toward them and, in an instant, he had gathered them up in his arms and was hugging them against his rough woolen sweater. He smelled as fresh as the salty sea air and his beard prickled Megan's cheek. Her heart was beating so hard she thought it would burst out of her chest.

"Let's have a good look at you two. I can't believe it! My little girls are all grown up." His eyes were watery and he was blinking hard.

"No, we're not, Daddy. Really, we haven't changed a bit. Not one bit," said Jennifer in her baby voice.

He grinned his lopsided grin and ruffled her hair. "Your carriage awaits, m'ladies," he said as he opened the rear door of the car and motioned them in with a sweep of his hand, like the chauffeur of a fancy limousine.

Megan climbed in and beckoned Jennifer to hurry. Her skin was tingling all over. When they were in, her father shut the car door and scanned the street nervously before getting into the driver's seat. Megan looked up and down the street too. Good. She didn't see anyone who would recognize them. No sign of Mrs. Persky and her precious Lana.

She bounced a little on the soft back seat, testing it. The passenger seat in front was piled high with groceries: a big bag of flour, a box of apples, cans of beans, beer, and more strangely, a large package of cloth diapers.

Her father grinned at them in the rearview mirror. "You two are certainly a sight for sore eyes," he said.

"I like your new car," said Megan.

"It's not really mine. Just rented, so don't make a mess. They check every little dent and scratch."

"Oh." Megan pulled her hands up into the arms of her jacket.

He switched on the motor and, with tires squealing, they took off into the traffic. Megan ducked as they approached the next corner. What if their mother was on her way to the mall and saw them? Or what if she had already discovered the note? Would she yell out, "Stop that car!" and call the police?

"Wait a minute," squealed Jennifer. "I don't have my seat-belt done up yet."

Their father slowed the car, but he didn't pull over and stop. "Give her a hand, Meg, will you please?"

"Holy tamales! If you'd set down those darn turtles, you could do it up yourself," she grumbled at Jennifer.

"Here. You hold them."

Megan slunk down behind her father's seat and held the turtle box until she heard the *click-click* of the seat-belt. She remembered how, when their father was living with them and they would go out in the car, she had always tried to sit behind him. It had felt as if she were on his side. Jennifer would sit behind their mother. That's how she always thought of her family: Jennifer and Mom were on one side and she and her father were on the other. Besides, she was tall and had his dark hair and eyes, while Jennifer and their mother had the same fluffy, blond hair and grey eyes. It was as if they were two separate teams.

After they had gone a few blocks, her father screeched to a stop at a stoplight.

"I've got something for you two in here, somewhere." He leaned over and rummaged through the parcels in the front seat. "They were on sale at the supermarket."

He pulled out two track suits folded up in plastic. "The small grey one is for you, Jen, and the medium navy one for Megan. Here are a couple of baseball caps to go with them. How about trying them on?"

He handed them back to the girls. The light turned green and he stepped on the gas again, racing the van beside him.

"You mean, put it on *now*?" asked Jennifer, frowning at the track suit.

"Yes," he told her. "Now."

"Change here? In the car?" Jennifer asked.

"Just slip them on over your shirt and shorts," he told her.

"But I'll roast," Jennifer protested.

Their father glanced back at them in the rearview mirror. Lines of tension formed around his mouth.

Megan shoved the grey track suit at Jennifer. "Just do it, Jen. You can open your window if you're too hot."

Jennifer reluctantly shook the track suit out of its wrapping. Megan ripped hers open. The suits were huge since they were women sizes, but Megan pulled off her jacket and pulled on the sweatshirt over her T-shirt, and rolled up the sleeves.

"Roomy," she said. "Nice and roomy." She helped Jennifer get hers over her head. She felt as if she were wearing a sort of disguise and she looked like a whole other person.

Soon they were whizzing over the Lions Gate Bridge on the way to the ferry terminal at Horseshoe Bay.

"Where are we going, Dad?" asked Jennifer. "Are

we going out to eat somewhere on the north shore like last time?"

"Hasn't Megan told you where we're heading?" he asked, keeping his eyes on the traffic.

"No. She just said we were going to meet you."

"I didn't get a chance to explain, Dad. Mom came home right after I talked to you."

Her father nodded. "Well, we're going to my new place. And I have a big surprise waiting there for you."

"A surprise!" said Jennifer. "Is it a new bike? My very own bike for my birthday?"

"Your what? Your own bike? No, no. It's nothing like that. You'll see. You'll see."

Megan was amazed Jennifer didn't beg to be told everything. Usually she was so impatient. When it was her birthday, she always had to know exactly what people were planning to give her. And she always sneaked around the bedrooms before Christmas, snooping for presents under the beds and in the closets.

"We're going on the ferry!" Jennifer squealed when they neared the terminal at Horseshoe Bay and drove into the lineup. "Is this the surprise?"

"No. This is on the way to the surprise," their father said.

While they waited in the car to board the ferry, he seemed awfully edgy, peering about nervously and glancing away whenever anyone looked in their direction.

Why don't people just mind their own business, Megan thought, slumping down in her seat, her baseball cap pulled low over her face.

After a while they drove onto the ferry and got out of the car. Jennifer's new track pants were dragging on the ground, so Megan told her to roll them up.

"Can't," said Jennifer. "I have to hold my turtles."

"Fine, I'll do it!" Megan stooped down and rolled the legs up for her. Then she squashed Jennifer's baseball cap down on her curls and turned her own cap backwards. "Come on. We can't stay down here," she said, shoving her forward.

They hurried up the stairs after their father, climbing from the car deck to the passenger deck.

"Sure am hungry," said Megan, smelling the french fries from the cafeteria.

"Me too. Me too," said Jennifer.

"Okay, okay. You talked me into it," said their father. "Let's have some lunch."

They stood in line with a tray and, when it was their turn, he ordered three hamburgers with fries, milk for the girls and a large coke for himself.

They sat at a small table beside a window. His hands were shaking so much that, when he lifted his cup, coke sloshed onto the table. Megan didn't think it had anything to do with the boat's rocking. He took a small green flask out of an inner pocket and poured a clear liquid into his coke. After he took a deep drink, his hands seemed steadier.

So he's still drinking that stuff, thought Megan. The last time they had seen him, he had told them that he'd quit drinking and joined AA, but it looked like he was back at it again.

Now that she was sitting across from her father, she could get a good look at him. He had changed a lot and it wasn't just the beard. He'd had a moustache before, but had always shaved his chin and trimmed his moustache neatly. Now his moustache almost covered his upper lip and a dark beard grew over his chin. His hair was much longer too. When he was working in the office as an accountant, he had looked like a businessman: neat and tidy, in a trim dark suit, tie and white shirt.

Now he was dressed as casually as a high school student or a truck driver. He wore rumpled, faded jeans, a plaid shirt with a frayed collar under a rough woolen sweater, and a padded vest, green on the outside and red on the inside. His old brown felt hat was pulled low over his forehead.

His dark brown eyes shifted about nervously. He'd always been a restless man, busy every waking moment. The only time she'd seen him relax was when he was watching a basketball game on TV.

He took another long sip and cleared his throat. "Now, let's take a good look at my beautiful girls," he said, his eyes searching their faces. Leaning across the table, he pulled off Jennifer's cap and tousled her mop of blond curls.

" 'Curly Locks, Curly Locks. Wilt thou be mine?' " he laughed. "I love your hair all fluffy like this. Makes you look like a kewpie doll."

"I'm almost eight now," Jennifer told him. "My birthday's next week. You didn't forget my birthday, did you, Daddy? Is that what our surprise is about?"

"Your birthday. Righto," he nodded. "I would never forget your birthday, Jenny."

He hasn't mentioned *my* birthday, thought Megan. Her twelfth birthday had come and gone last May without a word from him. She remembered sitting in the living room all evening, pretending to be working on an important science project, and refusing her mother's invitation to go out for a birthday supper. She was waiting for her father's birthday call, but it never came.

She took a big bite of her hamburger. When she tried to swallow, it got caught in her throat. Oh well. He had probably been very busy. May must have been right in the middle of a really hectic time at the office.

"And you, Meg, you're at least a foot taller. I like your haircut. Looks terrific. So what's new with you these days?"

"New? Ah, I made the senior basketball team at school."

"That's great! I bet you're the star."

She shrugged. She was only on the "B" team. She still had a hard time controlling her big flapping feet and her elbows were always in the way.

He grinned at her. "So far, so good," he said, wobbling his black eyebrows.

When he grinned at her like that, with his wide smile and the crinkles fanning from the corners of his eyes, she just had to grin back.

FOUR

When they got to Vancouver Island, they drove north from Nanaimo up the Island Highway.

"Are we there yet?" asked Jennifer. "Is this our surprise?"

"Not yet. Not yet," said their father.

After what seemed like hours, Megan grew tired of staring out the window at the blur of dark forest splattered by an occasional house and glimpse of the ocean. They went through a few small towns without stopping for anything except the red lights.

Finally they drove into a car rental shop on the outskirts of another small town.

"This is where we get out," said her father. "You two wait here while I pay the guy and get us a cab."

"Oh, no!" said Jennifer. "I just thought of something, Daddy."

"What?"

"We said we'd meet Mom for lunch at the mall. It must be way after one o'clock now. She'll be worried if we're not there."

Her father glanced at Megan, his eyebrows raised. Was he mad at her for making plans? She couldn't tell.

She shrugged. "Mom won't be really worried. She'll just think we're still at the library."

"But what if she calls the library? She'll find out there really wasn't a dinosaur show," persisted Jennifer.

"Tell you what," said their father. "I'll call her cell phone from inside the office. I'll tell her you two are with me and not to worry."

Jennifer nodded. "Okay."

"In the meantime, how about doing me a favour? Could you put these bags of groceries into the taxi when it arrives?"

When he had gone into the office, Jennifer said, "Do you think Mom will be really mad when we don't meet her?"

"I left her a note," said Megan. "So I don't think she'll be *that* upset. She'll get to have the whole long weekend to herself, to do whatever she wants. I mean, it's not like she spends a lot of time with us anyway."

"I guess," said Jennifer, but she didn't sound too sure.

"Just don't tell Dad that I left that note, okay?"

"Why not?"

"He'd be really mad."

Jennifer nodded. "Why? He said he'd call her anyway."

A taxi arrived before Megan could answer. It was dark blue with NORTH ISLAND CABS in white block letters on its dusty side doors.

The driver was a jolly man, short and broad as a pumpkin. "So you must be the young ladies awaiting your stagecoach."

Megan helped him move the bags from the green Toyota into the cab's trunk. "Come on. We need some help here," she said to Jennifer, who was sitting on the curb now, whispering intently into the turtle box.

"I can't," she said. "I've got to hold my turtles. Besides, I'm in the middle of telling them a story."

"You could put them down for a minute."

"I don't want them to get scared or lonely."

"Oh, we can manage," said the taxi driver. "There," he wheezed, after a few more trips. "That must be the lot. You've got enough stuff here to last you until the cows come home."

"We're visiting our dad," Jennifer told him. "We haven't seen him for ages and ages, and he told us he's got a big surprise for us."

"Well, well," nodded the taxi driver. "Is that right?"

Megan thought he was beginning to look too interested. She glanced toward the office, hoping her father would return before Jennifer told the taxi driver anything more, but there was no sign of him. She crouched down beside her sister and said, "What story are you telling your turtles this time, Jen?"

"Their favourite. You know, *The Tortoise and the Hare*. Only I changed it to *Two Turtles and the Hare.*

They like it better that way."

"Really? I don't think I've heard that one."

"I could tell it to you, if you want," offered Jennifer.

"Okay," said Megan, gritting her teeth.

"All right. I'll start it from the beginning then. It all started one bright sunny day ..."

At that moment their father appeared.

"What can I do you for?" the driver asked him.

"Take us to Murphy's Dock," their father told him and climbed into the back seat of the taxi, between the two girls.

On their way, Jennifer said, "What did she say? What did Mommy say when you called her?"

"Oh darn!" said their father, smacking his forehead. "I completely forgot. Look, I'll call her as soon as we get to the dock."

But when they got to Murphy's Dock, Jennifer forgot about the phone call in all the excitement about a boat ride.

Their father didn't remind her.

And neither did Megan. Her mom would be worried, but she'd find the note soon and they'd be seeing her on Monday.

"A boat ride!" squealed Jennifer. "Is that our surprise?"

"No, not really," said their father. "Now we need all this stuff loaded into that boat over there," he said, pointing down to where a dozen or so boats swayed in the water at the edge of a float. "Can you give me a hand again?"

The taxi driver helped them unload the boxes and

bags onto the wide wooden dock before collecting his fare and driving off.

Megan followed her father down a steep ramp to the float. Her arms were weighed down with grocery bags. She had avoided the diaper package. There could be all kinds of explanations for it, she told herself. Her father could have bought them for a friend's baby, or a neighbour's. That was it. He was probably delivering them to a family on a nearby island.

"Here she is," their father said, pointing to *The Irish Lass*. It was a small white motorboat, with peeling paint and four seats, two behind and two in front, with a steering wheel and a narrow windshield.

They made several hurried trips and stacked the boxes and bags on board. Their father was as edgy as ever, his shoulders hunched and his movements jerky. He kept glancing around as if he expected someone to jump out and arrest him on the spot.

Megan kept watch too.

A couple of teenagers and a woman who looked as though she might be their mother, brought their boat in and moored it at the float behind them.

"Good afternoon. Another fine day," the woman called out to Megan's father. "Great weather for the Thanksgiving long weekend."

"That's for sure," he said, ducking his head and rushing the girls onto the boat.

Megan pushed Jennifer aboard. "Hurry, hurry," she muttered under her breath. She slid into the seat behind the driver's so she'd be on her father's side again.

Jennifer didn't care about hurrying. She settled into the other back seat, cradling the box of turtles in her lap. She opened the box a crack and whispered to them. "It's okay, you guys. Don't you worry. We're just going on a boat ride. It'll be fun. You'll see. You'll love it."

"You should buckle on these," their father said, handing them a couple of orange life jackets.

"We're not going to tip over, are we?" asked Jennifer, her voice uncertain.

"No, no. Wearing life jackets is just good safety. Besides, they'll help keep you warm. It can get windy back there."

Megan clipped on her life jacket and helped Jennifer with hers. She wiggled into the shiny, blue plastic seat to get comfortable. It had a thin plastic-covered cushion but it wasn't much help.

"Where are we going?" asked Jennifer for the twentieth time.

"You'll see. You'll see," said their father again. He hastily untied the rope and started the motor. The boat slipped away from the dock.

"Hold on," he called out to them. "We're off."

The boat *vroomed* away from the dock. Soon the town disappeared in the white spray. Megan took a deep breath. They were almost there.

Jennifer stared at Megan, her grey eyes huge. She clutched her turtle box and looked so nervous that Megan almost told her where they were going.

Instead she said, "Don't be such a scaredy-cat, Jen. We're almost there. Relax."

But it was more than an hour of sneaking through narrow passages between densely treed islands, around towering cliffs and rocky reefs, then a long ride through open water where the waves splashed up against the boat's hull and washed over the side of the boat. Jennifer squealed when that happened.

"Don't worry," yelled their father over the roar of the motor. "It's just water. It won't hurt you."

Overhead flew a line of black birds, their long necks stretched out like winged broom handles.

"Cormorants," their father yelled.

The monotonous hum of the motor and the steady slapping of waves made Megan drowsy and soon lulled her to sleep. When the sound of the motor changed, she woke up. She didn't know how long she had been out.

The boat was approaching an island. It threaded carefully between jagged reefs in shallow water so clear that she could see the bottom. Long strands of green and brown seaweed swayed in the current. Sharp rocks broke the surface. She gripped the back of her father's seat, expecting the boat to run aground any moment. But he steered the boat slowly, steadily around the rocks, toward the shore.

Trees and bushes covered the island. On one of the tallest trees perched a large dark bird with a white head and tail. It stared down at them as regally as a prince. Then it stretched out its enormous wings and swept down off its high perch, skimming over their heads and screeching at them like an old rusty wheel.

"Our resident eagle," her father told them, "officially welcomes you to Eagle Island." He gave Megan a thumbs-up sign and grinned at her.

She grinned back. They were here! They had made it. The whole weekend lay ahead. She took a deep breath and stared up at the eagle until it glided out of sight.

Hidden behind another jagged reef was a small wooden dock, stained a dark green to blend into the surrounding foliage.

As they approached the dock, slowly now, the motor cut to a quiet *put-put*, Megan saw a small shed on the beach beside the dock, but she couldn't see any other buildings. Was that where her father lived? Surely not.

"Where's your cabin?" she asked him.

He glanced up into the bank of trees and bushes that were huddled on the edge of the beach. "Can't spot it from here, can you? All those fir trees and salal bushes totally hide it," he grinned as he manoeuvered the boat to the dock. He cut the motor and jumped out, hanging onto a rope that he tied around a short pole.

Rocky cliffs towered on both sides of the beach. The cliffs on the right were bare and jagged, whereas the cliffs on the left were covered with thick bush.

"Is this your surprise, Dad?" Jennifer asked, looking around. "Do you live here now?"

"Right. That's part of the surprise. Now come and see the best part."

Megan scrambled out of the boat and followed them up the dock. She leaped down onto the damp sand and looked around. The beach was edged with dark green bushes. She inhaled deeply. Green. That's what this whole place smelled like. The colour green. A delicious dark green. How different the air was from the smoggy city! And they were here! This was her father's place. They had finally made it. She felt like dancing across the beach and yelling "Yippee!"

"Bridget!" called her father. "We're here!" He wrinkled his brow. "Funny. She's usually down at the dock when I come in. You can see the boat coming into the bay from the cabin. Wonder where she is?"

"Bridget?" said Megan. "You mean that, that lady is here too?"

"You remember her, do you?"

Her stomach sank. The last time she had seen her father, months and months ago, he had picked her and Jennifer up after school and taken them out for supper at Ravioli's on the north shore. They had met his friend, Bridget, at the restaurant.

Megan remembered her, all right. She was a plump, round-faced woman with long black hair and such a thick Irish accent that most of the time you couldn't understand what she was saying. Not that she had talked much that night. All during supper, her eyes had barely left her father's face. She had stared up at him like one of the saints in church stared up at Jesus. Adoring. And Megan's father had been more cheerful that evening than she had seen him for a long, long time.

Maybe ever. When the waiter had asked if he wanted anything to drink, he had said, "No, just water, thank you. I've given up the drinking." That was a surprise because, until then, he would have needed no excuse to have a beer or a whiskey. His drinking was one of the main things he and her mother had fought about.

But what was that Bridget woman doing here — here, on her father's island?

Megan had thought that she was going to have him all to herself. She had thought that her father was going to make up for those empty months and months when he had been away.

Now she would have to share him with that Bridget woman! She had certainly not counted on that.

FIVE

Megan's father looked worried.

"Bridget!" he called again. "She can't have gone too far. The kayak is still up on the beach." He pointed to a long narrow red boat near the shed. "Maybe someone came over and she got a ride with them. But it isn't like her to just leave like that."

It had started to rain. Jennifer tucked her turtle box under her coat to keep it dry. "You still haven't called Mom," she said.

"Oh right. I'll have to zip over to the fish farm later and give her a ring on their cell phone. We'll just get this stuff up to the cabin and out of the rain. Grab a couple of bags each, will you, and follow me." He picked up a heavy-looking cardboard box from the boat, crossed the beach and disappeared into the thick woods.

Megan handed a plastic grocery bag to Jennifer and picked up two more herself.

A narrow trail cut through the green bush and trees and climbed steeply uphill to the top of the rocky cliff.

"Wait for me," puffed Jennifer.

But Megan didn't wait. She climbed steadily up the trail, ducking under branches, following her father.

At the top of the trail, she pushed through some bushes into a clearing and a neat wooden cabin with a wide deck appeared. A big tree with reddish orange bark peeling in long, shaggy strips screened the deck. Megan couldn't remember seeing such a strange tree in the city.

The deck had been built with fresh unpainted wood and was bordered by a low wooden railing. Five broad steps and a narrow ramp led from the gravely path up to the deck. The cabin itself was older and panelled in weathered grey wood. Megan followed her father up the steps and climbed over a low gate, the type people used at the top of their steps to keep small children from falling down the stairs.

A wooden picnic table stood in the centre of the deck. All sorts of stuff cluttered the tabletop: twisted driftwood pieces, pine cones, the remains of a bird's nest, a blue glass ball the size of Megan's fist and, in a chipped clay pot, a huge bouquet of colourful wildflowers: blues, purples, pinks and yellows. Her mother would scoff at such a riotous mixture of colours, none of them black and lacquered.

"Strange," said her father peering around the deck.

A galvanized washtub half full of sudsy water and a scrubbing board with a damp cloth draped over it, sat on a low table beside the screen door. Beside it was a pail of white clothes waiting to be washed.

"Very, very strange," he muttered. "It's not like her to leave the washing half finished."

Maybe she's gone, hoped Megan. For good.

She and Jennifer followed him into the cabin. He stopped so abruptly that they almost bumped into his back.

"What's that ...?" he said. He pulled off his hat and peered upward.

Megan followed his gaze. He was staring up at a large rectangular hole in the floor of the loft. She blinked in the dim light. Then she saw her.

Bridget was crouched at the edge of the hole. She was staring down at them, her arms wrapped protectively around a baby! A baby!

"Oh thank the Lord in heaven and all the Saints! It's yourself, it is?" the woman said.

There was enormous relief in her thick Irish voice.

"Of course it's me!" said Megan's father. "Who else were you expecting?"

"I thought it was that wild bear coming in to get us — me and the babe. True, I thought it was." Her voice trembled.

"But how? What the ...?"

Megan noticed that a ladder had been pushed over and had smashed into something beside a desk.

Her father rushed to the desk. "Oh, no!" he cried.

"Not my antique gramophone!"

"Sorry. I'm so sorry, dear," said Bridget from the loft, "but I thought the bear was going to climb right up here and grab us. So I — I kicked the ladder until it was loose, then I pushed it over. I didn't realize it would fall on your record player."

Megan's father sighed heavily. Megan held her breath, waiting for him to start yelling, "Of all the stupid, idiotic things to do!" But he didn't say a thing. He just shook his head and went to pick up the ladder.

"Want to give me a hand with this?" he asked Megan.

The record player was the old-fashioned kind; you had to wind it up using a crank on its side. When the ladder had knocked it over, a pile of records had spilled onto the floor. The records looked familiar. Megan recognized the operas: *Carmen* and *La Bohème*, her father's favourites. In the old days, no one had been allowed to touch them.

She helped him lift the heavy ladder up off the record player and prop it back up against the edge of the hole in loft floor.

When it was set securely, he asked Bridget, "Shall I come up and help you with Joey?"

Megan gasped. So this was her father's surprise! The baby was not just Bridget's. It was also his son! And he had named him after himself. Joey from Joseph.

It was bad enough having a woman here, but a woman who'd had Megan's father's child, his first son. That was too much! Megan felt sick. She clenched her teeth.

"No, no. I can manage just fine," Bridget was saying. Holding the child in one arm, she nimbly descended the ladder.

Megan's father took the child from her and cradled him so tenderly in his arms that Megan knew she had guessed the truth. Her insides wrenched. Now, she could never be his favourite. How could she compete?

"Girls, I'd like you to meet your brother, Joseph, better known in these parts as Joey. Named for his grandfather, Joseph, in Ireland, and for me, of course."

"Our brother? Really?" said Jennifer. "Let me see!"

The baby was quite fat with fuzzy dark hair and drool trickling from his mouth. He had been browned by the summer sun. He looked up at Megan with dark eyes fringed with stubby dark eyelashes. They reminded her of something. Or someone.

The baby snuggled into her father's shoulder, the right shoulder, which had always been *her* spot. Even Jennifer respected that. She did not like that one bit.

"Oh, he's so cute," squealed Jennifer.

Totally predictable, thought Megan. Jennifer said anything smaller than a bread box was "so cute," including those two disgusting turtles she was still clutching.

"And I'm sure you remember Bridget?" their father asked.

"Hello, girls. Welcome to Eagle Island."

Bridget was a tall woman and not at all as plump as Megan remembered. She had long black hair and fair skin with a spattering of faint freckles on her nose and cheeks. She looked younger than Megan remembered as well, definitely a lot younger than her mother. She was wearing a long-sleeved denim dress with buttons up the front and a purple sweater over her shoulders.

"Hi," said Jennifer. "We came over in the boat and the waves got so big they splashed right over the side."

"It can get pretty rough out there sometimes," said Bridget, nodding.

"And we saw a real eagle too," Jennifer went on.

"So tell us about the bear," Megan's father interrupted.

"I was just out there on the deck doing the laundry when I saw a branch move at the top of the cliff and it rose up out of the bushes."

"You mean the salal bushes at the bottom of the deck?"

"Yes. Well, I nearly died. My heart stopped still for a second. Then I grabbed our Joey from beneath the table and, before I even got to the door, the bear had risen up on its hind legs and was waving its long nose back and forth like a mad trumpet player. I didn't wait to see what it was looking for. I just raced in here, sure enough."

Megan's father looked alarmed.

Bridget went on. "Then I thought to myself that it might follow us right into the cabin, that glass door being so flimsy. So I scrambled up there into the loft with the little one. But then bears can climb trees, can't they? What would be stoppin' it from climbing right up the ladder? So, I kicked at it until it came free and pushed it over," she finished breathlessly.

"So I see," said Megan's father. "So I see. You don't think that was overreacting just a bit?"

"Overreacting?" Bridget's blue eyes flashed at him. "And what would you have me do? Stay out there on the deck and welcome that bear right into the cabin and invite it to stay for lunch?"

"No, no. Of course not. I mean, it didn't even come up onto the deck, as far as I can see, much less break into the cabin." He glanced over at his bashed-up record player.

"I'm sorry the ladder landed on your record player, Joseph. But I was terrified, I really was."

"Right," he nodded, his lips tense. Megan thought he was about to start yelling, but Jennifer interrupted.

"Daddy. You still haven't called Mom. Remember, you said you'd go out to the fish farm and call her?"

He turned from Bridget and sighed again. "I'll go as soon as I can. Don't worry."

"After all your travelling, you must be starving," said Bridget. "Let's see to getting some tea on and a bit of supper. I know I'm famished. I've been up in that attic since before lunch. And Joey needs his nappy changed." She started whirling around the kitchen.

"So who'd like to hold her new brother while I see to the record player?" said Megan's father.

Megan backed away, hands behind her back, shaking her head.

"Me, me!" squealed Jennifer. "Oh, can I?"

"Sure thing. Sit down here, at the table."

Jennifer wiggled herself comfortably into a wooden

armchair at the head of a long table. She put down her turtle box carefully and held out her arms, her eyes sparkling.

Her father gently placed the baby on her lap.

"Goo-goo, ga-ga," she said into his face.

He drooled and gurgled back.

Her father laughed. "You two speak the same language."

He went over to the record player and Megan followed. "My God!" he said, surveying the mess. "I guess we can start by getting the gramophone upright." He struggled to lift the cabinet.

"Here. I'll give you a hand," Megan said.

It was surprisingly heavy. They finally got it in place and he opened the lid to check the damage. He whistled softly, then proceeded to tinker with its insides.

"How come you've got such an old-fashioned record player anyway?" Megan asked him. "Why don't you just get a ghetto-blaster?"

"We don't have electricity on the island and this gramophone will work without batteries. You just wind it up with this crank. Now, can you hold this bit, and this?" He picked though the pieces of broken glass and wires. He didn't seem as angry as she expected. If anything had ever happened to his precious records or the stereo at home, he would have hit the roof.

"Guess we won't be listening to *Carmen* tonight," she said.

He shrugged and said, "Guess not. This is too big a job for the moment. Think I'll leave it and get the rest of those groceries up from the boat."

"I could give you a hand," she offered.

"That's okay. I'll just fill up the wheelbarrow. Maybe you could help Bridget with supper, though. There's a good girl."

She grimaced.

He pushed open the screen door and the wind slammed it shut behind him. She watched him disappear down the steps, into the swiftly falling dusk.

Jennifer was in the corner now, playing with the baby and his blocks and trucks.

Bridget glanced up at Megan from the smoking wood stove. "Oh, what a cold, wet night it'll be tonight!" she said.

"I don't mind a bit of rain," she mumbled, leaning against the wall beside the door, her hands shoved into her coat pockets. The cabin was cold and dank. Even with the rain, it was probably warmer outside.

"I'll just get this stove going and we'll be as cozy as can be in no time at all," Bridget said. "Then we'll have a spot of tea."

Megan didn't say anything. Her eyes stung from the smoke. She blinked and scanned the kitchen. The floor was made from dark oiled floorboards and the cabinets were a lighter wood with dark green countertops and open shelves above them. Bridget had lit two lanterns, one on the counter beside a sink with a small hand pump, and the other hanging over the long wooden table, where Jennifer and the baby were playing on a worn carpet.

Megan felt her lips twitch when she thought of what her mother would say about this kitchen. "Early Rustic" or "Backwoods Basic" or something like that. She wondered if her mother had found the note yet.

Bridget moved around the stove, feeding it bits of wood and muttering. It was a large old-fashioned wood stove with a compartment for the fire on the left and what looked like an oven on the right. A round stovepipe came out of the back and went up into the kitchen ceiling.

"Come on, old stove," Bridget said, digging around its insides with a poker. "Don't be stubborn as Donovan's donkey tonight." She pulled her cardigan closer around her shoulders and tapped her sandals impatiently. She poked inside again.

After a while, she turned to Megan. "There now," she said. "Looks like it's finally caught. This old stove can be a bit temperamental. Just like some people I know," she laughed. Her round cheeks shone pink in the lantern light and a stray wisp of dark hair dangled in her face. She tucked the hair behind her large ears.

Doesn't she know that when you have ears like that, you should try to keep them covered? Megan smoothed her own hair down over her ears as she remembered her mother's advice.

"Now. To warm up the soup," said Bridget, sliding a big covered pot to the left side of the stove where it would be closer to the fire. "Could you see to setting the table, please?" she asked Megan.

"I guess so. Where are the bowls?"

"In that cupboard beside the sink. We'll also need cups for our tea. Cutlery will be in that drawer."

Megan grunted. She set the table: four places, one on each side of the table. She hoped that she could sit next to her father. To get to the table, she had to step over Jennifer and the baby. They were right in her way.

On her third trip back to the table, carrying four mugs by their handles, she tried to step over the baby, but he put his hand out and she accidentally stepped on him, not hard, but hard enough to make him squeal in pain.

Before she could set the mugs down, Bridget had swept over and scooped him up.

"Oh, sweet baby, baby. What is it?" she cried.

His red face glistened with tears.

Jennifer said, "It was Megan. She stepped on his fingers."

"Sorry," Megan said woodenly. "I didn't mean to, but he was right in the way."

"Hum," said Bridget, looking at Megan, her eyebrows raised. Then she crooned to the baby, rocking him. "It's all right, little darlin'. It's all right."

Once in his mother's arms, he stopped crying almost immediately and hiccupped.

There was a rumble outside on the deck.

"Oh good. That'll be your dad back with the wheelbarrow," Bridget said.

The door swung open and Megan's father pushed in the wheelbarrow overflowing with parcels.

" 'Here comes Santa Claus, here comes Santa

Claus,' " he sang in a big hearty voice. He shook the raindrops from his hat and presented Bridget with a box of daffodil bulbs and a rose bush.

"Ooh, gorgeous! Daffs for our garden next spring. And a Peace Rose as well!"

"And, and, something else, very special for my queen," he said, rummaging around in the bags. "Ah ha!" He produced a handful of orange packages.

"Jaffa cakes!" Bridget squealed, hugging him. "My favourite! Brilliant! You're spoiling me."

Megan waited for Bridget to tell her father that she had trampled on the baby's fingers, but she didn't. She just said, "Looks like the soup's finally ready. Everyone sit down. With Jaffa cakes for dessert, it'll be a regular party."

After a supper of a thick potato and carrot soup and some home-made Irish bread, too crumbly to spread with butter, Megan suddenly felt enormously tired. It was as if a heavy blanket had settled upon her shoulders.

She was about to put her head down on the table when her father said, "Think it's time for bed."

Megan shook herself and got up.

"Good night now, you two," said Bridget. She was sitting at the table drinking tea and breast-feeding the baby.

"Good night," said Jennifer. She got her box of turtles from the counter.

"G'night," mumbled Megan, blinking. She left the table quickly because she was afraid that Bridget might actually expect a kiss good night, but Bridget didn't move from her chair.

Climbing up to the loft, Megan felt the sharp edges of the ladder rungs dug into her feet through the rubber soles of her basketball shoes. It was not a trip she'd like to make barefoot, that's for sure. Her father led the way, carrying one of the lanterns. It swung, casting drifting shadows around the room.

The loft was a wide, murky room with low, sloping ceilings. There were two bunks built into niches on either side of a big window. A round, braided rug covered the plank floor.

Their father put the lantern down on a low table in front of the window. Jennifer set her turtle box beside it.

"When you're all organized and ready for bed, just turn the lantern off with this lever," he told them.

Megan nodded.

He pulled the curtains closed. "That rain on the roof is your night music. A lullaby for my beautiful sweethearts." He hugged them both at once, Jennifer at his left shoulder and Megan at his right. Above his usual odour of salt and sea and beer, she caught a faint whiff of baby. She tried not to let it show on her face.

"Good night, Dad," she said.

When he had gone, she saw there was a T-shirt on each pillow.

"Guess we use these for PJs," said Jennifer, picking up hers.

Megan picked up the other. It was pink with white pansies across the top — obviously one of Bridget's. "I'll just wear my own shirt to bed, thank you very much," she said, disdainfully kicking the pink shirt onto the floor.

Jennifer looked at her with wide eyes.

Megan yanked off her shoes and damp socks. Her feet were black from the dye. She wiggled her black toes at Jennifer.

"Yuck," said Jennifer. "You should wash your feet."

"There's no shower, so how can I?" She shrugged and pulled off her sweatpants, shorts and sweatshirt and piled them on top of her shoes. Then she turned off the lamp, as her father had instructed, and slid into the sleeping bag.

In the light trickling up from the kitchen, she could see faint shadows of the rafters in the sloping ceiling. The wind was blowing the rain steadily against the roof. It sounded as if they were inside a giant drum.

"I think Bridget's really nice. And Joey's so cute, don't you think, Meg?" said Jennifer from her side of the room.

"Yeah, they're okay, I guess."

"But what about Mom?" said Jennifer. "Won't she be worried about us?"

"I told you, I left a note for her so she knows we're with Dad. And he did say he'd go to the fish farm and phone her tomorrow, first thing. He'll explain everything. No prob. So go to sleep now."

Megan curled herself into a comfortable ball with

the sleeping bag tucked around her shoulders. Almost immediately she grew warmer. Even her damp feet started tingling cozily.

Jennifer didn't say anything else, but after a while Megan heard a noise above the steady rain. The noise sounded a lot like Jennifer sobbing.

Reluctantly Megan uncurled herself and left her sleeping bag to creep across the cold ridges of the braided rug.

Jennifer was scrunched up, facing the wall.

"Okay. What's the matter?" Megan gently patted her sister's back until she stopped sobbing. "You don't have to worry, you know. Everything's going to be all right."

"But I'm scared, Meg," Jennifer sniffed. "We're so far from home."

"What's to be scared about? We're here with Dad and you said yourself that you liked Bridget. So what's the prob? Shove over, will you. I'm freezing."

Jennifer moved over and opened the sleeping bag so Megan could crawl in beside her. It was already warm. Megan put her arm around Jennifer's waist and held her close.

Jennifer hiccupped. "I've never been so far away from home without Mom before," she said. "Except for sleepovers at Judy's and that Christmas we spent at Granny's house, but Mom was with us then. She'll be so worried about us, Meg."

"I told you, Dad said he'd take care of it tomorrow. First thing."

"Really and truly? What if he forgets again?"

"He won't," promised Megan. Well, maybe not, she said to herself. She reached down to scratch her itchy foot.

Jennifer sighed and pulled the sleeping bag close around her shoulders.

It was too dark for Megan to see, but she knew her sister was smiling now. Soon Jennifer's breaths came in deep, even strokes. She was asleep.

Megan could have moved back to her own bed, but she didn't. As she drifted off to sleep herself, she dreamt she was dribbling her basketball in the driveway, passing it from one hand to the other, feeling its roughness under her fingertips, hearing the hollow sound as it bounced on the concrete. Her father was on the court too.

"Pass it here, pass it," he hissed.

She bounced the ball to him. He passed it back. She caught it and lunged toward the basket. She'd show him. She had been practising, waiting for this day. She threw the ball. *Whoosh*. Two points.

"Marvellous!" her father said, clapping. "Looks like you're ready for the big leagues." He caught the ball and bounced it back to her.

She was farther from the basket now, but still she wanted to take the shot. Maybe he'd want to come back and live with them and be her coach. She imagined she was the youngest player on Canada's Olympic team and he was their coach. They would be such a great team …

She aimed and shot the ball but, of course, it missed.

She wasn't concentrating. She wasn't visualizing the ball going through the basket. She was thinking instead of the crowd cheering as she scored that winning basket, of how everyone would hold her up on their shoulders because in the dying moments of the game she had won a gold medal in basketball for Canada and had made her father proud.

"Oh well," her father said, shaking his head sadly. "Practice makes perfect."

That's what he always said. But that's all she'd been doing these days. Every waking moment. Practising, practising, practising.

And she had failed him again.

SIX

Light flickered across Megan's face. Where was she? She jolted upright and bashed her head. She held her throbbing temple and looked around at the low sloping ceiling, the braided rug on the floor. Then she remembered.

She eased herself away from Jennifer, pulled on her clothes and shoes and climbed down the sharp rungs of the ladder.

Bridget was sitting at the kitchen table in the armchair, in the same position Megan had left her the night before.

"Where's my dad?" she asked her.

She saw the baby's small fingers tug at Bridget's long, dark hair. He was propped in the crick of her arm and she was breast-feeding him.

Megan turned away. It was embarrassing to watch.

She went to the door to look out.

"He's gone down to the woodpile under the deck to chop some wood. We need to light up the stove to get our breakfast started. You'll be wanting an orange or a Jaffa cake to tide you over until breakfast is ready, so help yourself."

"No, no. That's okay. I'll wait." Megan clamped her baseball cap on backward, pulled the door open and went outside.

At the edge of the deck, the green bushes were shiny and wet. Thick mist crowded around the cabin, blotting out the surrounding view and the tops of the nearby evergreen trees. It made her feel totally alone, as if no other land or sea existed. It was silent except for a muffled "thunk" coming from under the deck. She went down to investigate.

Her father was chopping wood. His axe was raised above his head. He took a quick breath and brought it down on a thick log propped up on the chopping block. "Thunk!" The axe bit into the wood, splitting it.

"Hi, Dad," she said, smiling at him.

"There you are!" He grinned back at her, tossing the split wood into the wheelbarrow. He was wearing his faded jeans tucked into rubber boots and a long-sleeved plaid shirt under his padded green vest. His brown felt hat was pushed to the back of his head.

"Need any help?"

"Glad you asked. Think you could run this load of wood up the ramp into the kitchen so Bridget can get breakfast started?"

"Guess so," she shrugged. She didn't really want to go back into the kitchen. Bridget would still be there. But she backed the wheelbarrow out and pushed it up the shallow ramp to the deck. She nudged the door open with her foot and, with a loud crash, tipped the wood into the box beside the stove. Out of the corner of her eye, she noticed the baby jump in his mother's arms, and he let out a wail.

"Oh, blast!" said Bridget. "And he'd just now fallen asleep."

"Sorry, sorry," said Megan. But she wasn't the least bit sorry.

Her father had chopped another pile of wood by the time she returned. "Thanks," he said, stretching his back and rotating his shoulders. "We'll just pile this load over there against the cabin."

"What are we going to do today, Dad?"

"Same as usual. Gather wood from the beach, chop it, pile it. Maybe work some on the deck. The outhouse needs a new roof."

Megan nodded. He didn't mention anything about going to the fish farm to call their mother.

"Breakfast won't be for a while yet," he said. "Bridget has to prod that old stove to life first. Sometimes that takes quite a while, but she's learning. We've got time to collect a load or two of driftwood and check out what the night tides have brought us."

Megan followed her father past the big tree with the reddish orange bark.

"Arbutus," he told her. "Grows only here on the

coast, close to the sea. Some people believe that if you rub its trunk, it'll bring you good luck."

She nodded and stroked the trunk where the bark had peeled away. It was a creamy colour, cool and satiny smooth under her fingers.

"Whoops. Watch your step here," he said.

Beside the bush on the path was a small mound of what looked like ground-up blackberries.

"Bear turd," he said. "Must be from Bridget's encounter yesterday. Not fresh anyway."

"Yuck," Megan said, stepping over it and following him down the trail.

"This bush here's salal." He pointed to the thick bush that the trail cut through. Under the leaves were tight clusters of black furry berries. "It's those berries the bears are after this time of year."

Megan looked around nervously.

"Don't worry," her father said. "No bears out here today."

Down at the beach, the tide had gone out and the sea had retreated to reveal a broad horseshoe-shaped beach, littered with a narrow rim of driftwood and strands of seaweed.

"It's here that you find the real treasures," he told her, poking at the seaweed with a stick. "It's the high-water mark from last night's tide. Once, I found a glass float right here."

"The blue one that's on the picnic table on the deck?"

"That's the one. It had probably travelled across the

Pacific Ocean all the way from Japan. Imagine. And it arrived here the very day Joey was born. What a gift!"

She wasn't sure if he meant the glass ball or his new son.

"Can't we do something special today? We're not going to just hang around the cabin and work all day, are we?"

"I've got to get these chores done now, but maybe tomorrow ..."

Tomorrow? Her empty stomach lurched. They'd be going back to the city tomorrow, wouldn't they? Had he forgotten? She was trying to think of a tactful way to ask him without making him mad when she saw the long, slim boat high up on the beach, next to the shed. "That's a kayak, right?"

"Right," he nodded. "Sweetest little craft ever invented. The Inuit surely had the right idea. It can go where no other boat can. How about a paddling lesson?" He looked at her, rubbing his hands together enthusiastically.

"Sure. I guess. When?"

"Tomorrow morning. First thing."

She nodded. Would they have time before heading back to the city?

Then she remembered. A long time ago, one really awful day at the park, her father had tried to teach her to ride her new bike. She just hadn't been able to get the hang of it. It was her sixth birthday and he had given her the bike that afternoon. It was lime green and speedy looking.

Her mother said it was too soon. "She's not ready," she had insisted. "We should wait." But they all went to the park anyway.

Her parents had already had a fight about her mother returning to work against his wishes. He wanted her to be a stay-at-home wife, like his own mother, a wife who would bake pies and make quilts and take care of her family. But that was not what Megan's mother wanted. She wanted a career.

Although her parents argued in hushed tones, Megan was very aware of the tension between them. She was so worried about how their fight would end that she couldn't ride the new bike. She was petrified of falling over, so she did. Over and over again, and she cried much louder than necessary, trying to draw her parents' attention and anger away from each other. But it didn't work. They just got angrier and angrier. And after one of her big squawks, everyone yelled even more loudly. Her father was so angry that he just threw up his hands and walked away, leaving them stranded. Her mother sat on a park bench, holding Jennifer on her lap, and Megan stood in front of her with scraped knees and elbows.

"Come on now, girls. We're going home," her mother said wearily. She got up and started to walk in the direction of their house. Megan didn't want to have anything to do with that beastly bike, so her mother had to drag it across the park with one hand and try to hold Jennifer with the other. "This thing's so heavy," she grunted. "You'll have to learn to control that temper of yours, young lady. You're getting to be too much like your father."

Although Megan had sensed that her mother meant it as a criticism, she had taken it as a compliment.

When they got home the bike was stashed in the garage and didn't come out for a long time.

Megan thought that was the day her father had left them, the first time. It had been all her fault because she couldn't learn to ride that stupid bike.

Would the same thing happen again tomorrow morning when they went out for a kayak lesson? Would she fall into the freezing water? Or would she be so scared that she would sit there paralyzed, not able to move? She twisted a reed between her fingers.

"Hey, Meg. Look at this," her father said, picking up a piece of driftwood and sitting on the log beside her. "What does it make you think of?"

"I don't know," she shrugged. It was just an ordinary piece of wood, bleached grey by the sun and sea.

"Something that sits on the top of the highest tree?" he hinted.

"An eagle, maybe?"

"Right! Just needs a bit of carving down here on the wing section and the neck." He pulled a red pocketknife out of his pocket and opened it. He started whittling the chunk of wood, shaving off thin chips until the back curved smoothly. The newly chipped wood smelled fresh and spicy. Maybe it was cedar.

"Want to give it a try?" He gave her the wood and the knife.

They felt warm in her hands.

"When you carve wood, always stroke away from yourself," he instructed. "Right. That's the way. You've got it."

She nodded.

"Always be aware of where your other hand is. You don't want to end up carving it by mistake," he laughed.

She grinned at him.

"Now take small chips out, small shavings. Here. I'll show you." He took the knife back. "This way you'll be less likely to make a big mistake and wreck your whole carving. It's safer too. Want to try again?"

"Sure."

He gave her the knife and she tried again. She felt clumsy with him watching her so closely.

"That's right," he encouraged. "Practice makes perfect."

She took small, light strokes. Tiny slivers of wood came away from the driftwood.

"Increase the pressure just a little," he said before getting up and continuing to check the beach for other bits of driftwood.

She pressed down harder on the blade, stroking, cutting into the wood. Soon she had built up a rhythm. She turned the wood in her hand, working on rounding the bird's shoulders, shaping its pointed tail, narrowing the neck slightly.

"Great. You've got a real talent, Meg. I can tell," her father said over her shoulder.

She felt herself glowing. "This is fun."

"There are two things about my island paradise that

makes carving the perfect hobby: lots of raw material and lots of time. You keep the knife, but better wear it around your neck so you won't lose it."

"Thanks, Dad." Around her neck, she slipped the long green cord that was attached to the knife and it dangled almost to her waist.

"Look. Here's another interesting bit of wood. A chickadee, maybe?" He reached behind the log and picked up an oval piece. "And what about that one over there?"

"A snake," she said. "A rattlesnake."

He pursed his lips and nodded. "Bridget's most feared thing."

"Is that so?" She really wasn't interested in anything about Bridget.

"They don't have any snakes in Ireland, you see. The story is that St. Patrick came and chased all the serpents out of Ireland because they symbolized evil. So you won't find a single wild snake anywhere in the whole country." He picked up the long twisted stick and waved it in her face. "S-s-s-s."

She laughed and scooted away along the beach while he chased her.

They combed the beach for all sorts of interesting shapes and chucked them into the wheelbarrow until it was full to the brim. As Megan was tossing in one last piece, she heard the sound of a motorboat.

Her father was chopping a log. He froze, his axe in midair, and listened as the sound of the motor grew louder and louder. A boat was coming into their bay and approaching the beach. An angry frown clouded his face.

"Get up into the salal!" he hissed at her. "And stay there. Now!"

Why hide? But her father was so stern that she dared not disobey him. She crouched down in the underbrush beside the path where she had a good view of the beach and surrounding water.

Her father, still holding his axe, crept down to a large rock at the water's edge and ducked behind it. He watched the motorboat approach.

It drifted closer and closer. It was quite a fancy boat with a high bow. It stopped and dropped anchor into the deep water several metres from shore. Some people scrambled into a dinghy and started paddling toward the beach: a man, a woman and a small child. A dog yapped excitedly.

Before they reached shore, Megan's father emerged from behind his rock and stepped out into the shallow water. He called out to the people in a loud rough voice that she didn't even know he had. "Hey you! This is private property. This whole island. No trespassing."

The rowing stopped. The three people and the fluffy white dog turned their faces to stare at him.

"We were hoping to come ashore for a picnic," the man called out. "Stretch our legs a bit."

Megan's father moved his axe up to his shoulder menacingly. "Like I said. Absolutely no trespassing." He took a step toward them in the shallow water.

The man and woman stared at each other. Then the

man turned the dinghy and paddled hastily back to their cruiser. They all scrambled aboard and motored away.

Megan's father stayed down on the beach until the boat was well out of sight. When he joined her at the path, his face was flushed and he was panting.

"Darn tourists. They think they can just take over any place they want. No respect for a man's private property, his private domain."

"But they just wanted to have a picnic."

"That's what they say." He narrowed his eyes at her. "But they really came to snoop around. Spies. I could tell." He dropped the axe into the wheelbarrow and pushed it back up the trail to the cabin.

She followed close behind. She had never seen him so riled up over such a small thing. Maybe he was right. Maybe those people *had* come to snoop. Maybe all kinds of people came here to snoop around but those people surely hadn't look like spies to her. They had looked like an ordinary family.

She dragged the long snake stick, drawing a crooked line with its tail, all the way up the trail to the cabin. Her father dumped the wheelbarrow load of driftwood under the deck.

"The wood will keep dry here," he told her, his voice back to normal. "We'll chop it up and pile it later. I figure we'll need this whole space under the deck packed full of wood for the winter.

"Holy tamales!" It was a huge space, the whole length of the house and several metres deep and higher than her father was tall. "Does that mean you're planning to spend the whole winter here? You're not going back to your apartment in town?"

He nodded. "I'm thinking of giving it up. It's a bit expensive to run two places."

"Won't it get too cold way out here?"

"That's why we need all this firewood. Oh, there's your eagle." He picked up the driftwood she had started to carve and handed it to her.

Holding its sloping wings, she said, "Think I'll smooth down his beak, make it flatter and more pointed at the end."

"Good plan," he grunted, pushing the wheelbarrow back to the path. "Let's go back down for more firewood."

She put her carving on the deck steps and followed him back to the beach.

The cruiser had not returned. Her father grunted and started filling the wheelbarrow again.

She began to feel like a puppy, following her master around. She followed him back up to the deck, unloaded the wheelbarrow, down to the beach, loaded up the wheelbarrow, back up to the deck, unloaded the wheelbarrow, and back down to the beach again.

Finally, Bridget called them in for brunch.

SEVEN

In the centre of the kitchen table was a mound of grilled cheese sandwiches on a large platter, a bowl of pickles and another of sliced carrots and celery. Megan's mouth watered.

Jennifer was already sitting next to their father's place, so Megan had to sit on the stool at the foot of the table. She wiped her hands on her sweatshirt, feeling the bulge of the pocketknife tucked inside, and helped herself to a sandwich.

She nibbled the warm and crunchy crust which was a bit blackened on the edges, then stuffed the whole thing into her mouth.

"I've made you girls a bit of cocoa," said Bridget. "Jennifer said you liked that better than tea." She poured the steaming liquid into Megan's cup. "Watch now, love. It might be a wee bit hot." She gave some to

Jennifer as well.

"Thank you," said Jennifer politely.

With her mouth full of sandwich, Megan couldn't say anything. She nodded her thanks and reached for another.

"Hold on there," said her father, popping open a can of beer and taking a swig before pouring it into his mug. "Don't be so greedy, Meg. Let everyone else have one first."

Bridget returned to the table smiling at Megan, the teapot and a package of Jaffa cakes in hand. "All that fresh air and hard work increases your appetite. Have another sandwich, love. There's plenty here and I can always make more."

As Megan's father was piling his plate with a sandwich and some vegetables and pickles, Bridget said, "Joseph, Jennifer tells me she's worried. Very worried, she is, that her mother won't know where they are. Does that mean Patricia didn't know they were coming here for a visit?"

He took a big gulp of his beer and coughed. He wiped his mouth on his sleeve and cleared his throat. "Right. True. She didn't know, but we were going to phone her. Right, girls?"

Megan nodded and came to her father's rescue. "That's right. We were going to do it when we got to the car rental place, but we forgot."

"But the poor woman will be off her head with worry," said Bridget. "She'll think the girls have been kidnapped or that something terrible has happened to them. You should have asked her before taking the girls."

Megan shook her head at Jennifer, in warning. If Jennifer told their dad about leaving the note, he would be furious with her.

"She wouldn't let me take them," he said. "I did ask, but she said, 'No, it wasn't convenient.' She wouldn't let me see my own daughters! My own flesh and blood!"

"Still, you know you must call her today. She'll be so terribly worried."

"I know. I can go over to the fish farm after we eat. As soon as I have that roof repaired on the outhouse."

"But surely the outhouse can wait."

"I don't think so. Looks like we might be in for another spell of rain before the day's over and it's leaking already."

He glanced out the window to the cliffs near the sea. The early morning mist had vanished into a thick, cloudy sky.

"A leaky roof is nothing compared to a mother's worry about her children," Bridget persisted.

"All right. All right. I said I'll go as soon as I can." He slammed his mug on the table, spilling beer on his clenched fist.

Bridget flinched at his anger, but went on. "So that's why the girls arrived here without a stitch of clothing except what's on their backs. I should have realized." She shook her head. "I could spare a couple of shirts and maybe a pair or two of tights if you two aren't fussy."

"It's okay," said Megan. "What I've got on is fine."

"But you'll be needing a change before long."

Megan shook her head.

The grilled cheese sandwiches sat like a lump in the pit of her stomach.

After lunch Megan went out to the deck to work on her carving. It still looked more like a kid's bathtub toy than a real bird. It needed more neck, she decided. She flicked open the knife and started to carve, shaving off slivers as her father had shown her. She could hear Jennifer chatting away with Bridget while they washed up the dishes.

Her father had gone up to repair the outhouse roof after all. Although he had invited Megan to come along, she thought that the smelly outhouse was one place she wanted to avoid. She much preferred the small chemical toilet in the closet behind the back door.

"Our mom sold over a million dollars in kitchen and bathroom renovations last year," she overheard Jennifer telling Bridget.

"Did she now! She must be a very good saleswoman."

"She's really an interior designer."

"Ah. And does she enjoy it?"

"Oh, yes. She's even designing *our* house. Right now everything in our kitchen is black. Even our new fridge."

"My, my. I've never heard of a black fridge."

"Now she's looking for a black stove to go with it."

"Well, they surely didn't have anything like that in

Dublin. At least they didn't when I was living there."

"When was that?"

"I've been in Canada almost five years now. Came to work as a secretary at your dad's office."

"Don't you miss your family?"

"Not much family to miss now that my own dad's gone. It's just my ma and one older sister. I'd love to go back home so they could meet Joey though. They would love him to bits."

"He's sure cute, all right."

They chatted on and on while Megan worked on her carving. After a while Bridget came out onto the deck with a basket of clean, wet towels and diapers to hang on the clothesline.

"These nappies might not dry before the rain comes, but I'll take my chances," she told Megan as she laid the diapers over the clothesline, which soon sagged under their weight.

Megan grunted in her direction, but she kept her eyes on her carving.

"My heavens!" said Bridget. "Where ever did you get that sharp knife?"

"My father gave it to me," Megan told her.

"Ah, that man!" Bridget shook her head. "Sometimes I wonder what gets into him. Mind that you be very careful now. It looks dangerous. I don't want you to cut yourself."

Megan didn't say anything. She didn't even look up at Bridget. She just concentrated harder on her carving until Bridget had gone back into the house.

Megan's father worked all afternoon on the outhouse roof. When it was time for supper, he dragged himself up the deck steps.

"Phew!" he said, mopping his brow and opening a can of beer. "That was some job!"

Jennifer was sitting across from Megan at the picnic table, making a bed for her turtles with Megan's wood chips. "You didn't go to the fish farm and call Mom yet, did you, Dad? Are you going to go now?"

He took a long drink of his beer and shook his head. "Too late to go now, Jenny. It'll be dark soon. It'll have to wait until first thing tomorrow. Maybe when Megan and I go out for our kayak lesson."

That night Megan tossed and turned in her sleeping bag. She knew she was going to fail tomorrow when her father tried to teach her to paddle the kayak. It would be just like when he'd first tried to teach her to ride the bike. Besides, she was really starting to worry about getting home. She had agreed to spend the weekend with him, but now it was starting to look as if he didn't plan to take them back any time soon. She would have to try and talk to him about it tomorrow.

"Jen," she whispered, "are you awake?"

Silence.

"Honestly. I don't know how some people can just fall asleep any old place and time they want to," she muttered. "Jen. Are you really asleep? Jen!"

She drew the sleeping bag up around her neck and turned to the wall. When she took a deep breath, a vision of her mother crept into her head: she was sitting at the kitchen table, her long fingers encircling her coffee cup. Would she be sitting there now, worrying about them?

She heard a sound outside, just below the cabin, in the trees. It must be Bridget's bear, back for more berries!

She got out of bed and crept to the window. Something was moving about in the bushes, but it was not a bear. Back and forth in front of the cabin, paced a dark figure with an axe on his shoulder and a bottle in one hand.

"Joseph," she heard Bridget's voice. "Joseph, love. Won't you come in now? It's late."

"Hush!" hissed her father. "I'm just checking these bushes." His words sounded slurred.

"But, why? Nothing's there."

"I thought I heard someone down here. Trespassers."

For a long time, Megan watched her father patrolling the trail. She watched until her eyelids grew so heavy, she couldn't keep them open any longer. She slipped back into her bed and fell into a troubled sleep, dreaming about axes gleaming in the moonlight and kayaks dumping into the frigid sea.

EIGHT

The next morning, glistening whitecaps rolled in the black water as far as Megan could see. Waves crashed onto the island, plastering the jagged rocks with spray.

"Are you sure it's a good day for a kayak lesson, Dad?" she said. "Just look at the size of the waves out there." She leaned on the windowsill beside his desk and pressed her nose against the window. The glass fogged up from her breath and her view of the crashing sea faded.

"What waves? Those are just swells. It's a great day for a paddle." Her father took a long drink from his glass. "Besides, I need a break from staring at this darn gramophone. I told Jennifer that we'd paddle over to the fish farm and make that phone call."

"Isn't it almost time to get ready to, um, take us back to the city anyway?"

He looked very disappointed in her. "Why, Meg? Aren't you enjoying it here?"

"Sure. Of course, I am. The island's great. It's just that … oh, I don't know." She shrugged.

"Well, it might be too rough to make the crossing to the fish farm in the kayak. It can get really choppy way out there in Dogfish Channel. Know what I mean?" He wiggled his eyebrows at her and grinned.

She tried to smile back, but something stopped her. She knew he wasn't planning to make that phone call. Rough seas or not. And now it looked as though he wasn't going to take them back to the city at all!

"You'd better borrow my paddling jacket," Bridget told Megan at the door. "That kayak is a wet boat so you can get soaked right through, especially in the front cockpit."

"It's okay. I've got my own jacket." Megan tried not to screw up her nose at the thought of wearing *her* clothes.

"Bridget's right, Meg," said her father, "You'll want to stay as dry as possible so you won't get cold."

They insisted, so she pulled Bridget's yellow kayaking jacket on over her head, but Megan held her breath so she wouldn't have to breathe in *her* smell. The jacket arms dangled over her hands and it hung down to her knees. "It's way too big," she complained.

Her father smiled at her. "Looks great, Meg. Now you look like a genuine kayaker."

He took the baby from Bridget's arms and they all headed down the trail to the beach.

Jennifer was walking in front of Megan. "Wish I could go paddling too. You're so lucky."

"You really want to go?"

Her sister nodded enthusiastically.

"Okay by me. Here's the jacket." Megan wiggled out of Bridget's jacket and slipped it over Jennifer's head.

When they got down to the beach, their father turned around and looked confused. "What's this?"

"Jen wants to go for a paddle first."

Her father shook his head. "Maybe later, Jen. Right now it's Megan's turn." With one arm around the baby he pulled the kayak jacket up over Jennifer's head. Then he handed it back to Megan with a smile. "You'll love it. I promise."

"Yeah, yeah." She knew all about his promises.

Her father and Bridget lugged the boat down to the water's edge where the waves licked at the hull. Megan could not imagine how such a flimsy-looking craft could actually be safe in those big waves, in that deep water. It was so narrow she could straddle the middle. It looked like a child's toy.

There were two open holes, one toward the front and one in the back, that her father called the cockpits. They were where the paddlers sat, he explained. And there were two other holes for storage, which were covered with lids.

He nuzzled Joey's neck and the baby giggled. "Okay, Meg o' me heart," he said, handing the baby to Bridget.

"Before you hop in, pull this on." He gave her a black rubbery garment.

"Looks like a skirt," she said, pulling it up to her waist so that it fit snugly and flared out around her hips.

"That's exactly what it is. A spray skirt. Keeps the water out of the boat. Once you've got your life jacket on, you can hop into the cockpit."

Jennifer was playing peekaboo with Joey around Bridget's back. He giggled every time she popped up beside him.

Megan took a long time doing up her life jacket. She sensed her father was becoming impatient. He was ready to go.

"Let's get cracking," he said, clapping his hands. "You sit in front and I'll be right behind you."

"Oh, no! What if I steer us into a rock or a cliff or something."

He laughed. "You don't have to worry about steering. I'll take care of that from the rear. Enough dilly-dallying now. In you hop."

Megan splashed through the cool shallow water. Shivering, she stepped into the kayak and gingerly lowered herself onto the low seat. It was molded plastic and padded with a sort of spongy material. She stretched her legs straight out and rocked back and forth.

"Comfy?" her father asked.

She nodded. "I guess."

"You'll find a footrest to brace against down there. Okay? Now attach your spray skirt around the cockpit rim. That's right. When a wave comes over the hull, no water can get into the boat, so you'll stay nice and dry. Here's the paddle." Her father handed her a long double-bladed wooden paddle. "Hold it tightly with your right hand and loosely with the left. Let the paddle just slide and roll between your thumb and your palm. Easy does it."

She nodded again. She tried to concentrate and take in everything he was saying, but her brain was mushy with worry.

What if the boat flips over and we get dumped into the sea? What if we can't make it back to shore? We'll drown. That freezing water will rush into our lungs and we'll both drown. She clenched her teeth to stop them from chattering.

"In you go," her father said, shoving the boat into deeper water.

Her heart lurched and pounded. She gripped the paddle in both hands.

"Remember, I told you to hold the paddle tightly with one hand, loosely with the other," he repeated.

"Which hand?" She couldn't remember anything.

The boat wobbled in the waves. She was sure it was about to flip over. This was worse than trying to learn to ride a bike, a lot worse. The worst you'd get learning to ride a bike was a scraped knee. She caught her breath and squeezed her eyes shut, waiting to be dumped.

But the boat didn't tip over. She cautiously opened her eyes. She was still upright!

"Okay," said her father. "Hold on. I'm getting in now."

The boat wobbled even more while he climbed into the rear cockpit. Although her heart was pounding, she kept her eyes open and, amazingly, the boat still didn't tip over. She took a deep breath and tried to calm down.

"Now," he said from behind her. "Are you holding your paddle in your right hand?"

"Yes." She held it up for him to see.

"And loosely in the left. Okay, reach out with your right. Drop the blade into the water and pull back. Then do the same with the left hand. Right, left, right. Great! You're doing it!"

"Good for you, Meg!" cheered Bridget from the shore. "You're brilliant!"

"Way to go!" squealed Jennifer.

A smile crept onto Megan's trembling lips. "You mean that's all there is to it?"

"That's it. You're a natural! A true kayaker. I've never seen anyone catch on so fast!"

She felt herself bristling with pride. She stretched her arm straight out and dropped the paddle blade into the water. Then she dragged it back. The pointy front of the boat cut through the waves.

Two black birds with long orange beaks and orange legs squawked loudly at them. She wondered if they thought they were actually singing. Maybe they were cheering for her too.

"Oystercatchers," her father said. "They hang around here all the time. Okay. Think you're good enough to paddle out of the bay?"

"Paddle way out there?" Her voice squeaked. "You

mean away from shore? I don't know about that."

"You'll be fine. Just fine. Don't worry. Paddling where it's deeper is no different from paddling here in the bay where it's shallow. A man paddled a boat like this one all the way across the Atlantic Ocean. No problem. And the Inuit have been using kayaks for centuries."

"Okay, I guess."

"We'll be back in a couple of hours," he shouted to Bridget and they headed off.

"Okay, Captain. Which way? Left or right?" he asked Megan when they got out of the bay.

"Right, I guess. But how do I turn this thing?"

"Just keep paddling straight on. I control the turns with the rudder and foot pedals back here. Steering is a piece of cake."

The boat's nose veered right and followed the shore instead of crashing into the rocks as she expected. It was still misty on the water and, in the distance, the wooly mist melted into the grey ocean.

Her father steered the boat around jagged rocks and reefs that were encrusted with black clams and barnacles and draped with green and brown seaweed.

On the highest rock sat an eagle. It turned its white head and stared down haughtily at them. As they drew nearer, it stretched out its wings and glided over their heads, creaking its strange, rusty cry.

"Must be guarding our island," said her father.

Megan nodded.

"So how do you like Eagle Island? Isn't it paradise?"

"Sure is," she agreed.

Frothy waves crashed against the cliffs. Shrubs and trees with reddish orange bark grew out of every possible crack and niche.

"Arbutus," she muttered to herself. "And salal."

"And Bridget and Joey? Aren't they wonderful? I knew you would get along."

At the mention of Bridget, Megan screwed up her nose and stuck out her tongue. She kept looking straight ahead so her father couldn't see her face.

When she didn't answer, he said, "She was really looking forward to your visit."

"Really?" muttered Megan. She bent to paddle. "Really."

"See that island over there?" He pointed to a mass of land across the water.

"Yes." She nodded.

"That's Goose Island. Here it is on the chart."

She turned around to see that he had strapped a chart in a clear plastic case to the kayak hull.

"When the tide's high, there's a passage between Goose Island and our island deep enough to paddle through. It's a great shortcut because we don't have to go way around Goose to get to Dale Point at the northern tip of my island. On the other side of Dale Point is Dogfish Channel and across the channel is Drack Island where the fish farm is."

"That's where you work sometimes?"

"Right. They raise fish from fingerlings in these big net pens slung in the water. Atlantic salmon, mainly for restaurants in the city. It's pretty interesting. We'll go over and check out the passage, but I doubt if the tide's high enough at the moment to let us through."

As they paddled toward what looked like a break between his island and another high mound of land, Megan could see that a low, narrow neck of land connected the two islands.

"Just as I thought," said her father. "The tide's still too low. Want to paddle around Goose?"

She was about to answer when she heard the drone of a motorboat in the distance. The sound became louder as the boat drew closer.

"Paddle hard, Meg! We'll duck behind that reef over there."

She paddled harder as her father steered the kayak.

"Okay. Stop paddling now." He grabbed the reef that was slimy with seaweed and crouched behind it.

She ducked down as well. Could it be the police searching for them? Maybe their mom had found out where the cabin was and had called the authorities.

The motorboat drew closer and closer. She held her breath. Should she call out and try to get their attention? It might be her last chance to get away from this island. Before she could make up her mind, the boat sped past, spraying out a white feather of foam.

"It's just Peter from the fish farm," her father laughed. "Must be on his way to town to pick up supplies. Don't know why he's heading for our place though." He pushed the kayak off the reef and hailed the motorboat. "Peter!" he called, raising his paddle. "Hey, Pete! Over here!"

But it was too late. Peter had not seen them. Their kayak bounced against the rocks in the boat's wake and they watched it until it had cruised out of sight.

"Oh, well. Bridget will take a message."

Megan nodded. "Are they the only other people who live around here? No other neighbours?"

"Right. Peter and his wife live at the fish farm full time. And a couple of other fellows come up from town to help out sometimes. I used to go out to give them a hand with the fish, but when Peter found out I was a chartered accountant, he asked me to do his books, so that's mostly what I do now. It's a good break and we can use the extra money for groceries and gas. I can earn enough to keep us going."

"Do you and Bridget go over to visit them very often?"

"No. Bridget has met Peter, but she hasn't met his wife yet."

"Why not?"

For a moment her father didn't say anything. Instead, he pushed the boat away from the rocks and started paddling. He cleared his throat and said, "It's just a matter of time before Bridget does meet her, I guess. But meanwhile, she's happy enough, living on the island with just Joey and me. And now with you two to keep her company, she'll be even less inclined to leave the island and go off visiting. I think we could live here alone forever. Don't you? No interference from the outside world. Just our family. Our own perfect island paradise. Know what I mean, Meg?"

She didn't really know what he was talking about, but she nodded anyway. As she suspected, it sounded as if he planned to keep her and Jennifer secluded here on his island as well. Like for how long? Indefinitely? Maybe forever? That was not at all what she had in mind when she had agreed to meet him. She had wanted to visit him, even spend the weekend with him, but to be forced to stay here, away from school and all her friends, that was more than she had bargained for.

"What about us, Dad? What about Jen and me?"

"You two are part of my family, Meg. Part of my island paradise. Of course you'll stay."

"But what about school? What about the basketball team?" She searched for the words that would convince him that he *had* to take them back to the city, back to their mother.

"I have that all figured out. You two can easily work on your school work by correspondence. They'll send out the course work. And we have piles of books at the cabin. We'll all be happier this way. You do see that, don't you?" His voice was eerily calm and quiet.

A chilly shiver crawled up Megan's back. The day had turned cold and bleak.

NINE

Megan inhaled deeply and concentrated on stretching out her arm and pulling the left blade back through the water. She tried to ignore the painful blister forming between her thumb and forefinger.

Those reefs were familiar. That even looked like the same eagle at the top of the tall spruce tree, standing guard. And were those the same oystercatchers hanging out on the cliffs? As the birds squawked their strange call, their long beaks opened and closed like pairs of bright orange scissors.

"That's the stuff, Meg. Reach as far forward as you can, then pull back. You're doing very well. A real natural."

She glowed at her father's praise. If only she could push away that dark seed of uneasiness in her chest. If only he weren't acting so weird.

She heard Bridget's voice float over the water. "Joseph! Peter came by. He wanted to talk to you."

Megan scanned the shore. There she was, hurrying across the beach, baby bouncing on her hip and her long black hair streaming behind her. She set the baby down on the sand and nodded to Jennifer to keep an eye on him. Jennifer's face was creased with worry, but she started playing patty-cake with him nonetheless.

Bridget splashed into the shallow water, holding up her long skirt. She caught the front of the kayak. "Now how was your paddle then?" she asked Megan.

"It was great," she nodded. Especially without *you* there, she added silently to herself. She lifted her paddle out of the water and held it high while Bridget tugged the boat's nose up onto the beach. Megan peeled the spray skirt from the cockpit, and Bridget held the boat steady between her knees while Megan boosted herself out.

Bridget was wearing that ugly hair band again, the one that revealed her large ears. As Megan stepped down into the shallow water, she flicked out her own hair to be sure her ears were well covered.

"So I guess you two didn't make it across to the fish farm?" said Bridget.

"No. The tide's still too low, so we would have had to go way around Goose," said her father, scooping up the baby and tickling his tummy with his beard so his voice muffled. "Too long a paddle for Meg's first time out, with those tricky westerly winds starting to blow up."

The baby dribbled sand from his wet mouth. "Oh, no, no, little fellow. Don't eat the sand. No sand in your mouth," his father said, gently wiping the baby's lips with his shirttail. He set him down beside Jennifer again and ruffled his hair.

Megan wasn't happy about all that affection. She frowned as she waded up to the beach, the cold water splashing around her knees and soaking her shoes and pant legs.

"So what did Peter have to say?" her father asked Bridget.

"He saw smoke last night on the north side of the island. Looks like there are campers over on Dale Point."

"What!" He dropped the paddles with a clatter and stared at Bridget. "Squatters on *my* island! Who do they think they are anyway?"

"They were probably just boaters who needed a place to camp overnight to get out of the weather."

"But it's private property. No one has any business squatting on my island. I'm going over there to give them a piece of my mind."

"Peter said he already checked on his way over here. There was some equipment left behind, but the campers were nowhere in sight."

"They'll be back. You mark my word. I've got to put up more NO TRESPASSING signs, make some kind of barricade with driftwood and rocks. I'll set out right now and stay the night. Catch those squatters red-handed. No messing around." He rushed to the dock and his motorboat, his eyes wild.

"Can I come with you, Dad?" Megan asked, pulling off her wet shoes.

"No, Meg. Might be dangerous." He barely looked back. "The girls will be fine with you, Bridget, won't they?"

"Yes, of course. But do you have to go?" She glanced at the bushes surrounding the beach.

"Surely you're not still worried about that bear!"

"Well, I just hope he won't decide to pay us a return visit."

"Keep close to the cabin. You'll be fine. You worry too much, Bridget."

"Do you really have to go, Dad?" Megan tried to keep the whine out of her voice.

"Of course, I do. Can't you see that?"

"But what are we supposed to do when you're gone? There's nothing to do around here."

"There's plenty to do. This is the great outdoors. And you could always give Bridget a hand."

"But we came here to spend time with you. Not her," Megan said to his back as he boarded the boat.

He swirled around and stared at her straight in the eye, his dark eyebrows furrowed angrily. "I'll be back tomorrow, if not sooner. You'll be fine until then. You're a big girl now."

"Okay, okay," she backed down. His sudden anger scared her.

Bridget said, "Don't forget to motor over to the fish farm and phone Patricia. Tell her the girls are safe with us."

"Right, right," he said, in a loud, angry voice. "You don't need to keep reminding me."

Megan knew that calling their mother was the last thing on his mind. She watched him thump about the beach, more and more frantic with each step.

"Joseph," Bridget said, holding his sleeve. "You'll be needing some food and water, and a sleeping bag if you're staying the night."

"Right. You're right. Of course," he nodded. "And tools. I'll need the saw. And my axe. Okay. Let's go up to the cabin." He scooped up the baby and led the way up the path through the trees.

They went single file, Megan's father, a tall king leading his troops. The baby was perched on his shoulders, drooling sand into his hair. Bridget followed closely behind them, swishing her wet skirt. Jennifer had to trot to keep up. Megan trailed behind, a long way behind.

Why should she rush? She and Jennifer were being left alone on a deserted island, away from anywhere and anyone, with a stranger. And their closest neighbours were on some distant island at a fish farm, whatever that was.

Her father was acting stranger by the minute. He just wasn't thinking straight. How could he think that keeping them secluded and isolated on this island indefinitely, maybe forever, keeping them prisoner, would be something they would actually *want*?

"What have I done?" she asked herself. She knew it wasn't all her father's fault that she and Jennifer were stuck here. It was her fault too. She had gone along with his plans. She had agreed to meet him. She had even lied to her mother. But she hadn't known that his plans for them involved more than just a weekend visit. And then there was Bridget and the baby. She had certainly not counted on *them*.

She hunched her shoulders and followed the procession up the path, dragging her bare feet in the sand.

Bridget was throwing together a hasty meal and packing it into a canvas bag while Megan's father pumped water into a plastic container. He stuffed a sleeping bag on top of the food, shouldered his axe and box of tools, and made for the door.

They all trailed after him down the path. Megan's toes dug into the sand with each step. Fat clouds had rolled in, covering the sun, and the sea had turned a dark purply green. She picked up her snake stick and dragged it behind her, gouging out a zigzag gash from the cabin all the way back to the dock.

"My birthday party," Jennifer was telling their father. "Don't forget it's my birthday tomorrow."

"Birthday?" He shook his head. "As if I'd ever forget such an important day, my Jenny. I'll be back tomorrow night at the latest, and we'll have a special birthday celebration for you then." He tossed his gear into the motorboat. "Now, give us a big hug." He wrapped his arms around Jennifer and Megan at the same time. "You two behave now. I know you won't give Bridget any trouble."

His arms around their shoulders were coiled with tension.

"You really won't be back until tomorrow night?" Megan mumbled into his sweater.

"Probably. That should give me enough time to deal with those freeloaders." He released them and pounded his fist into his hand. "I'll teach those troublemakers a lesson they won't soon forget."

Megan nodded. She stared at the waves while he kissed Bridget goodbye.

He hugged the baby too. "Keep him safe." He started up the motor and waved as the boat sped out of the bay. "See you soon," he called into the wind.

His jaw had been clenched and his eyes smouldered. Megan was glad that *she* was not the object of his anger. She idly kicked at a rock. They lingered on the dock until they could no longer hear the motor. Even the raucous oystercatchers who had been chasing each other on the cliffs were gone.

Bridget broke the silence. "Well, now. I'm off to do something with the rest of Joey's laundry."

"We'll stay down here on the beach for a while," said Megan. "Want to, Jen?"

Jennifer shrugged.

Bridget peered around the dock, checking the bushes and the cliffs. "Should be all right," she said. "But if you see anything at all, run straight up to the cabin quick as you can."

Megan knew she was worried about that stupid bear, but they hadn't seen any sign of it except for that mound of droppings beside the deck.

She wandered along the beach, kicking through the

fringe of seaweed left by the falling tide, hunting for an interesting piece of driftwood. Jennifer trailed behind her.

"Bridget's nice, don't you think?" she said.

Megan grunted.

"She keeps reminding Dad to phone Mom. Mom must be really worried about us. I bet she might even call the police if she doesn't hear from us soon. Wonder why Dad hasn't called her yet. It's almost as if he doesn't want to."

Megan grunted again. She held her breath, yanked off Bridget's smelly paddling jacket and chucked it toward the kayak. The cold wind caught her between the shoulder blades. She would rather freeze than wear *her* jacket.

"Want to build a sandcastle or something?" she asked.

"Sure. Should we build it down here by the water? We could dig a deep moat around it with a drawbridge and everything."

"Okay." Megan heaped sand into a pile and patted it down while Jennifer dug a narrow moat around it with a flat stick. While water from the sea trickled into the moat, Megan found some rocks and shells to decorate the castle's walls and a twig with strands of seaweed clinging to it to stick into the top for the flag.

"Here. You can use this board for the drawbridge."

The sun peeked out from between the clouds for a moment and warmed Megan's shoulders. She stretched them. They were a bit stiff from the long paddle. She found some small twigs and put them around the courtyard for stick-people.

"You know Bridget's like our stepmother, right?"

"Guess so," said Jennifer, shrugging.

"Well, you know about stepmothers, don't you? They're all evil," Megan said, narrowing her eyes.

"You're wrong about Bridget. She's not evil. She's kind," Jennifer insisted. "I like her. I really do."

"That's how much you know. What about the stepmother in *Hansel and Gretel*? At first they thought she was nice too, all that candy, but then she turned out to be an evil witch. What about *Snow White*? And *Cinderella*? And have you ever heard the story about the swan children?"

Jennifer shook her head. "Who are the swan children?"

"They're four children in an Irish folktale whose stepmother was so jealous of them that she cursed them and changed them all into swans. They had to wander the earth for hundreds and hundreds of years, never finding peace. According to the legend, that stepmother had long black hair and a snow white complexion. Just like Bridget."

"That's just a fairy tale," scoffed Jennifer, putting the driftwood over the moat.

"Right. But in every story, there's a grain of truth. Have you ever heard a story about a *good* stepmother?"

Jennifer looked up at her with fear in her eyes. "I'm going back up to the cabin. I'm sure you're wrong about Bridget," she said, heading up the trail.

Megan shrugged and went on patting the castle

walls. She told herself that she didn't care. She didn't care about anything. She nudged at the driftwood bridge and kicked over the castle, stomping on it until it was gone. She walked along the edge of the water, kicking at rocks and driftwood. Finally, she brushed the sand off the front of her shirt and wandered up the trail to the deck and unhitched the low gate at the top. She plunked herself down at the picnic table under the arbutus tree and fished out the pocketknife to continue carving.

Jennifer was crouched on the floor with the baby, showing him her turtles. He was like her own private windup toy. "Now this one's Tweedledum," she was telling him. "Tweedledum. Can you say that, Joey?"

He gurgled at her, touching the turtle's back with a wet forefinger.

Bridget came out of the cabin, heaving a large basket of clothes. "Ah. That baby gate's been left open," she said, frowning. "Remember to keep it closed, girls. We don't want our Joey tumbling down those steps and breaking his neck."

"Yeah, yeah, yeah," Megan muttered. She flicked out the longest blade in her knife.

When she made no move to shut the gate, Bridget sighed impatiently. She set the basket down with a grunt and shut it herself, before hanging up the wet clothes, draping white rectangles over the line.

"If you two have anything to wash, I could do it for you now while there's still enough warmth in the day to start drying them," she offered.

"No, I'm okay," said Megan.

Jennifer said, "I have a couple of things. I'll go up and get them."

Megan began carving, turning the lump of wood in her palm, stroking it with the blade, smoothing out the rough spots, getting the feel of it. She started on the bulge in front where the beak was going to be. A sharp, wicked beak. She carved off flakes and slivers that drifted to the floor. She scraped at the wood with steady strokes. Sometimes the knife hit the tabletop and nicked a gash into its surface.

The baby crawled over to her. He pulled at her pant leg with his damp fingers and hauled himself up, as if he was trying to inspect what she was doing.

She wrinkled up her nose. Phew! What a stink! Did his diaper ever need changing! She pulled her leg away and he sat down hard.

He whimpered a little, then picked up a bit of wood from the deck.

She kept her eyes on her carving and ignored him.

Just as he was putting the wood shaving into his mouth, Bridget swooped over.

"No, no, little man. Not in your mouth, love. Not in your mouth," she said as she tossed the shavings over the railing. "Ah, so it's a new nappy my little man's needing." She swept him up in her arms and kissed his slobbery chin. "Oh, Megan, I wish you would use a block of wood to do your carving. Our table is getting to look worse than your dad's old chopping block with all those scratches and nicks on it."

Megan tightened her lips and didn't say anything. She glared up at her until Bridget flinched and looked away, embarrassed.

"We'll just get you cleaned up, little fellow," she murmured and carried the baby into the cabin. The screen door slapped shut behind her.

Forgetting for a moment that she didn't have any shoes on, Megan kicked the table leg hard, smashing her big toe. She clenched her teeth at the pain and gripped her knife in her fist. She plunged the blade deep into the picnic table.

Jennifer came out of the cabin. Her jaw dropped when she saw Megan's knife sticking out of the table top.

Megan glared at her in the same silent way that she had glared at Bridget. Then she turned away to stare out through the fluttering arbutus leaves at the horizon, out to where the grey clouds met the grey sea.

After a while Bridget opened the door. "Come on in and we'll have some lunch," she said. Her voice was calm. "It's getting too cool to eat outside."

Megan wrenched her knife out of the table top, snapped the blade shut and followed Jennifer inside. She avoided Bridget's eyes and Bridget didn't say anything about her gouging the picnic table.

"What about my birthday tomorrow?" Jennifer asked Bridget. "Can we still have a birthday cake even if Dad isn't here? My mom always has one."

"Oh course, love. I don't see why not. I'll make you my special blackberry cream cake. There's nothing finer. You'll see. And do you know it's going to be our Joey's birthday as well? Well, not quite. Eight months he'll be. Not that he'll even know."

"Have you and Dad lived up here the whole time, ever since Joey was born?"

"We came out here in the spring when he was a couple of months old. I didn't know at first how I'd manage with no electricity or washer or anything, but it's all worked out. And all this fresh air's so good for Joey." She clucked him under his chin as he drooled applesauce down his bib.

She continued to chatter away in a false "let's cheer up, everybody" kind of voice. "After lunch I'll put him down for his nap. Then Megan, you and I can go up behind the house and pick some blackberries for Jennifer's cake."

Megan started shaking her head. "But, but what about the bear?" It was the only excuse she could think of to get out of being alone with Bridget. She couldn't say that she was going to bike down to the mall to meet her friends, or shoot some baskets in the driveway, not on this desolate island.

"Mmm. You're right," said Bridget. "But we'll be very quick about it and we'll have a good view from the hill up behind the cabin so, if we do see him, we can rush back here."

After they cleared the table, Bridget took the baby for his nap. Megan followed them to the bedroom and leaned on the door frame. She didn't want to go right in.

It was a big room, all yellows and blues. The wide double bed was covered with a sunflower spread. On the low windowsill stood a statue of the Virgin Mary in her flowing blue robes. Megan scraped the side of her right leg with the sole of her left foot and stared at the statue.

Bridget pulled a filmy blue curtain across the window to block the light and the view of the sea, before laying the baby in his crib. It was in a corner beside a low chest of drawers stacked with folded diapers and towels. Bridget leaned over the crib and gently patted the baby's back, crooning a lullaby. The slats of the crib made faint shadowy lines on his cheeks.

When he was settled Bridget wound up the base of the Virgin Mary and a tinkly melody, an old hymn maybe, lulled him to sleep.

Bridget put her finger to her lips and she and Jennifer tiptoed out of the room.

Megan went out to the deck, closing the door quietly behind her.

A few minutes later, Bridget came out with two bowls.

"There now. He should sleep for an hour, maybe even two if we're lucky. Ready to go blackberry picking?"

"But you shouldn't leave him alone, should you? What if he wakes up?"

"Jennifer will see to him. We'll just be up behind the house."

Jennifer twirled out onto the deck. She was practising her ballet again. "What do I do if he wakes up?" she asked.

"Just give us a shout. We won't be far, just up there behind the outhouse. But you mustn't pick him up, all right?"

Jennifer nodded.

"You might want to borrow my shoes, Meg," said Bridget. "Yours are soaked and the rocks are awfully sharp up on the cliff."

But Megan shoved her bare feet into her own wet high-tops by the door. She didn't bother tying them. She clomped down the steps after Bridget, her loose laces hissing angrily. She dragged her heels, creating little puffs of dust.

She picked up her snake stick again and drew another long zigzag gash on the path. This time the line wound its way behind the cabin, skirted a weedy, unkempt vegetable patch, went past the outhouse with its new green roof, and stopped at the base of some high rocks covered with blackberry vines. The whole time, Bridget kept chattering.

"We've had a grand summer for berries, all this heat, but I think this will be the last of them until next year. Have you ever had a fresh blackberry cream cake? I never tasted anything like it back home. It's brilliant, it is."

Was Bridget trying to fill the emptiness with talk about nothing? Was she feeling that emptiness too? Megan paid as much attention to her as she would to a flock of squawking birds.

"I have a jar of huckleberry preserves left over from the summer. We could mix that in with the blackberries. Wouldn't that be delicious?"

Megan didn't say anything, but Bridget didn't seem to need an answer.

"I'll make the cream layer and put it down near the well in the pumphouse. It'll keep cool there and be out of the bear's reach." She looked down toward the water. Megan followed her gaze past the bushes, past the cabin, to the water's edge. Not even a chipmunk in sight.

Bridget chatted on and on in her lilting Irish singsong. Her voice reminded Megan of a Steller's jay that liked to raid the hazelnut tree under her bedroom window. "Jay, jay, jay," it would call, waking her up too early.

Bridget told her about when she was a student living in Dublin. There were two terrible dogs that guarded the front yard of her flat, so she always had to sneak out the back way. She still had nightmares about those brutes. "At least there are no stray dogs here on this island. We can be thankful for that."

Megan saw her shiver. She didn't think it was because the wind had picked up. She wanted to tell her that she didn't have to keep talking, but Bridget seemed to think Megan needed entertaining.

She tried to get away from her chatter by moving off to another bush higher up the hill, but Bridget just followed her, gabbing away, laughing at her own jokes. Well, she had to, because Megan sure wasn't going to laugh at them. Laughing was the last thing she felt like doing.

They moved still higher to where the blackberry vines were growing in an impenetrable mass against the steep cliffs. Megan reached between the thorny bushes for an extra big, scrumptious-looking berry and the thorns scraped the back of her hand. She popped the berry between her lips and crushed it against the roof of her mouth with her tongue, savouring its sweetness.

"You want to check these berries, first," said Bridget. "Sometimes they've got a wee green worm inside."

"Yuck!" Megan coughed out the berry.

Bridget laughed and went on picking. And talking.

Megan saw her snake stick lying where she had left it on a flat rock. "Look out! A snake!" she yelled, pointing at the stick.

"A snake!" Bridget screamed. "God have mercy!" Dropping her bowl, she pushed Megan aside to face the attack herself.

But the snake didn't move. She peered more closely at the rock.

"Oh, Meg! It's just a stick!" she grinned. "What a joke! My heart's racing like a steam engine! Thank God, it's only a stick." She stooped down to gather the spilled berries and went back to picking and chattering.

TEN

Their bowls were only half full of blackberries when Megan heard Jennifer yell.

"Bridget!" The wind carried her voice up the hill. "Joey's awake and he won't stop crying."

"Oh dear," sighed Bridget, frowning. "And we don't have near enough berries yet. I wanted to pick the high ones before the birds got to them. Maybe I shouldn't have left Jennifer to look after him. She's so young."

Although she didn't come right out and say it, Megan knew that Bridget wanted her to go down to the cabin and check on the baby.

"Want me to go?" she asked. Anything to get away from this woman's constant chatter.

"Would you? You're a darling, Meg."

Megan put her bowl on a rock and galloped down the hill to the cabin, leaping over shrubs and tussocks.

"He woke up and now he's crying and crying," said Jennifer waiting at the door. "He wouldn't stop even when I tried playing peekaboo with him." Her face was red and her curly hair was in a tangle.

Megan rushed into the bedroom, Jennifer close behind her.

"Now, now, now. What's the problem? Hush, little guy. Hush, hush, hush." Megan leaned over the side of the crib and patted the baby's back.

Tears streamed down his blotchy, red cheeks. He wouldn't stop crying.

"We could try winding up the Virgin Mary again," Megan said.

Jennifer wound it up again, but the tinkly music didn't help either. He put his arms up to Megan, begging to be picked up.

When Megan reached into the crib to lift him out, Jennifer said, "Bridget said *not* to pick him up."

"She told *you* that, because you're too small. I'm old enough to pick up a baby."

She lifted him out of the crib and grunted. She hadn't expected him to be so heavy. Or so wiggly. Or so smelly!

He arched his back away from her and she stumbled and lost her grip. She tried to grab him more tightly, but he jerked out of her arms and fell, bashing his head on the corner of the dresser. He slumped to the floor and began screaming in earnest.

"Oh, no!" Megan gasped. She clapped her hands over her mouth and stared aghast at the blood gushing from his forehead and streaming down his cheeks.

"You dropped him!" Jennifer bawled. "He's really hurt! You dropped our Joey! Do something!"

For an instant Megan was too stunned to do anything but stare and feel horribly sick to her stomach. "What have I done?" she thought. She swallowed hard and held back tears. She turned and stared at the doorway, wishing Bridget were here. But the doorway was empty.

"Jen! Run and get Bridget! Now!" she shouted over the baby's howls. "Tell her it's an emergency."

Jennifer dashed from the room, calling to Bridget.

Megan could hear her frantic voice even over the baby's howls. "Bridget! It's Joey! He's hurt!"

She grabbed a diaper from the dresser and tried to hold the baby and press the diaper to his head to stem the blood, but he wouldn't let her near him. He cowered away and let out high-pitched screams.

Although it was probably only a minute, it seemed like hours before Bridget finally swooped like a whirlwind into the bedroom.

She seized her baby in her arms. "Ah Jaisus, Mary and Joseph! My babe! My poor wee babe! What's happened to him?" She held him close, folding her arms around him as if to ward off further injury. She grabbed the diaper from Megan and held it firmly against his head, pressing him against her chest and rocking him. She stared at Megan, tears welling up in her eyes.

It was as if Megan had injured *her*, had bashed *her* over the head.

"I'm sorry," Megan whispered. "I'm so sorry. I tried to lift him up, but he wiggled away and ..." She broke off. There was no excuse. "I didn't mean ..."

And then she was in Bridget's arms too. And so was Jennifer.

"I know. I know you didn't mean to hurt him," murmured Bridget. "I know." She rocked them all back and forth and took a deep breath, sobs catching in her throat. "Hand me his blanket from the bed," she urged. "There's a good girl." She bundled him up in the soft blue blanket and dabbed his forehead again. "Oh, sweet Jesus! It's a deep gash. So much blood. We need help," she said, more to herself than to the girls. "Help. It's help we're needing."

She gathered up the baby in his blanket and rushed to the doorway, but then she stopped abruptly as if it had just occurred to her that there was no help on this island. Joseph was gone and so was the boat. There were no next-door neighbours to rush to, no doctors or nurses, no hospital. They were completely isolated, completely alone.

She scanned the room frantically, her eyes wild. "Phone!" she gasped. "We'll phone for help." Still clutching the howling baby she stumbled toward the old desk. There was no phone.

Jennifer followed her, panicking as well.

Megan held back.

"Oh, how I wish your father were here!" Bridget shouted at them over the baby's head. She rocked him on her shoulder, gently rubbing his back, but he still wouldn't stop howling. He clutched at his mother's hair. She bit her lower lip, blinking hard.

Megan had an enormous lump in her throat.

"Maybe a bit of juice would help calm him." Bridget struggled to cut open a juice container with one hand.

"I'll do that," offered Jennifer.

"Oh thank you, love."

Jennifer fought to open the juice box and pour some into the bottle.

Megan watched her struggle but didn't move to help her. She couldn't. She felt paralyzed, stuck to the floor.

Bridget nodded her thanks when Jennifer finally handed her the bottle. She sat at the table and tried to get the baby to drink. At first he wouldn't have anything to do with it and turned his head away, wailing. Finally, Bridget was able to force the nipple into his mouth, and then it was very quiet while he frantically gulped down the juice.

"There. There. That's better, darling. That's better," murmured Bridget, holding him close, her fingertips caressing his chin.

When he had drained the bottle, she lifted him to her shoulder and gently rubbed his back. He started to cry again and burped up all the juice.

"Yuck," yelped Megan in spite of herself.

Jennifer got a towel and handed it to Bridget.

After she wiped up the juice, she paced back and forth in front of the kitchen stove. "I just don't know what to do. What *can* we do? Oh, if only your father were here!" she said again. "But he'll not be back 'til tomorrow night." Her voice trembled and she struggled to keep control. "We've got to get help. All this blood! Stitches. He'll be needing stitches to close that gash. It might be worse. It might be concussion. I don't know. I just don't know."

Megan waited for Bridget to blame her, to tell her it was all her fault. She had dropped him. Not that she had *meant* to hurt him. Had she?

But Bridget didn't stop her frantic pacing for even a second.

"I'll go and get Dad," Megan blurted out. Her lips felt frozen. She took a deep breath and forced them to move. "Jen and me, we'll go and get him. Now. We'll go right now."

"What?" Bridget stopped and stared at her as if she were crazy. "But how can you? He's way over on the other side of the island. There's no way to get there from here. Too many steep cliffs. The thick bush. All those brambles and salal. We can't get there. The only way is by boat and he's got the boat. We're stuck here alone until he gets back. And by then, by then ..." Her voice trailed off as she buried her face in the baby's blanket.

Megan stared at her. Her insides twisted. "We'll take the kayak," she said. "And paddle around. We can do it. Right, Jen?"

Jennifer looked at her with huge frightened eyes, but she nodded all the same. She picked up her turtle box from the counter.

"What the ...?" Megan began.

"I can't leave Tweedledee and Tweedledum here all by themselves." Jennifer's voice wobbled and her eyes grew even bigger. "They'd be too lonely. Too scared."

Megan grabbed her jacket off the hook by the door and shoved it at her. "You'll need this. Come on. We have to go! Now!" She snatched up her own jacket and pushed her sister out the door.

"But Megan," said Bridget to her back. "All that way around the island to the north end in the kayak. Do you think you can make it?"

"We can do it," Megan said firmly. "We have to."

The screen door slammed shut behind her.

She desperately wished there were some deep hole she could crawl into and disappear. Since there wasn't, she would have to climb into that flimsy boat and paddle out into the waves all the way to Dale Point. She *had* to.

She scooped up her eagle carving from the picnic table and stashed it in her coat pocket. They were going to need all the luck they could get.

She hurried Jennifer across the porch and down the steps.

Bridget followed them outside. The baby was crying still, his howls muffled. She had draped a rain poncho over her head, covering the baby in her arms, and they all stumbled down the path.

When they got to the beach, Megan grabbed the front of the kayak. "Grab the back, Jen," she grunted. "Good, the tide's high now," she said, as they half dragged, half carried the boat down to the water. "We should be able to take that shortcut between Goose Island and Eagle Island now."

Jennifer just stared at her. Megan knew she had no idea what she was talking about. She was so scared that she wasn't even listening. If Megan could have left her behind and gone on alone, she would have, but she needed her. Someone had to paddle in the front cockpit. And that someone had to be Jen. There was no one else.

The wind had quickened, lashing the sea, stirring up the waves into foaming whitecaps. A storm had appeared out of nowhere. Rain dashed into the steely sea and the wind howled, blowing gritty sand into Megan's face, her mouth, her eyes. She squinted against the grit and dashed back up the beach to the shed.

"Now the life jackets and paddles and stuff," she muttered. "Here, Jen, grab these." She heaved the two long paddles at her.

Jennifer stashed her turtle box under her jacket and fumbled for the paddles.

Megan dragged the life jackets and spray skirts down to the kayak. She was panting now, breathing hard.

"Are you sure you can do it, Meg?" Bridget asked again. "I'm sure you shouldn't be paddling out there alone."

"What else can we do? Wait until tomorrow night? By then it might be too late."

"Maybe I should go."

"And leave the baby with us? We wouldn't know

what to do with him. Besides, you need two to paddle this boat."

Bridget was still shaking her head, looking frantic with worry.

"Dad said I was a natural. Remember? Paddling's easy. I can show Jen what to do and we'll stay close to shore."

"If only we had a proper boat," said Bridget.

"Dad said a kayak's a great boat. The Inuit have been using it for centuries."

"But still ..." It seemed that Bridget couldn't think of any other argument.

Megan helped Jennifer pull on the spray skirt and life jacket. Then she quickly yanked up her own skirt and, with frantic fingers, buckled on her life jacket. She held the boat steady in the water while Jennifer climbed into the front cockpit. Megan splashed through the shallow water and helped her attach the spray skirt to the cockpit hole. Her fingers felt as if they belonged to someone else. They wouldn't work properly.

"There. That should do it," she said finally. "It'll be okay, Jen. Really. I promise," she tried to reassure her sister. "Dad and I, we paddled almost all the way to Goose Island this morning. And then we paddled back. It didn't take that long. It was simple. It'll be a piece of cake. That's what he said. A piece of cake."

Jennifer blinked fast and nodded. She was trying hard to be brave. But when Megan handed her the paddle, she gripped it with both hands, and her fingers were like small, desperate claws.

Megan gave her tousled hair a reassuring pat and climbed into the back cockpit herself. Fumbling, she attached her own spray skirt and stretched her legs straight out until she found the foot pedals.

Still holding the whimpering baby in one arm, Bridget shoved the boat into deeper water until it was floating freely. A wave hit the kayak broadside and it lurched, dumping water on them. Megan gasped and grabbed the hull.

Bridget stumbled as the wave splashed her, soaking her and the baby. He screamed as she clutched him. "There, there, little man," she murmured. "It's nothing, just a wave." But he kept wailing. She stumbled back through the water, up to the beach, her wet skirt clinging to her legs. She checked his bandage. It was soaked with bright red blood. "Ah, dear God," she murmured and held him close, her eyes shiny.

Megan gulped hard and took a deep breath. She dug into the water with her paddle and pulled back hard. She struggled to hold back the sobs that were lodged in her throat. "Come on, Jen," she barked. "Start paddling. Now! We've got to get there fast! Right, left. Reach out with the paddle as far as you can and pull it back through the water. That's right."

The boat's nose cut through the waves, slowly gaining momentum.

"That's great, Jen! You've got it. You're a natural. A natural paddler!" She heard echoes of her father's voice in her own.

The water in their bay was so clear she could see down to the rocky bottom, to the swaying seaweed and the starfish. The boat veered back and forth while she struggled with the steering pedals. It seemed to take forever to get out of the bay, but they finally made it.

"All right. I think I've got the hang of this steering." Her words were blown away by a blast of wind. A dense sea fog, thick as cotton candy had rolled in over the water and a fresh wind had churned the water into a chop. The surrounding islands were half hidden in the mist.

"I can't see anything out there," Jennifer shouted. "How are we going to find that Goose Island?"

"I know it's somewhere to the left. We'll follow the edge of our island to that headland sticking out ahead. Then we just keep going straight. You ready?" Megan shouted above the sound of the wind and the crashing of the sea on the cliffs beside them.

She thought Jennifer nodded. She dug her paddle into the choppy waves and pulled back hard just as a huge swell rolled toward the boat and crashed over the hull, soaking them both with freezing water.

Jennifer squealed while Megan gasped and clamped the paddle tightly with both hands. The boat settled back into the water.

"Calm, now. Be calm. Deep breath," she told herself. "You can do it. You can do it." She concentrated hard on reaching forward as her father had taught her, as far forward as she could, straightening her arm at the elbow. She dug into the water again and pulled back. Spray flared up in her face and she blinked it out of her eyes. The salt stung her lips. She bit them and kept on paddling.

She felt the boat moving forward now. As long as they were within sight of their island, she knew they were making progress because she could see they were pulling away from the rocky bluffs.

"Are we almost there?" Jennifer shouted.

"That's the headland I was telling you about up ahead. See it?"

Jennifer nodded.

"We'll paddle up to that spot and then we should be able to see Goose Island on the left. The tide should be high enough to take the shortcut between the two islands."

"But how can you tell? I still can't see any island out there. Can you?"

"It's out there all right. The fog is hiding it. We'll see it when we get closer. It's not so far. Come on now. Let's paddle as hard as we can."

"My arms are aching."

"The more you paddle, the quicker the ache will go away. Just remember to stretch your arm further forward with each stroke."

Megan paddled straight out into the chop. She paddled for what seemed a very long time, but might have been only minutes. Although she dug the paddle into the water and pulled back as ferociously as before, she had no sense of movement. She could have been in a gym, working out on a rowing machine.

"We aren't getting anywhere!" Jennifer yelled back.

"Sure we are."

A gigantic wave crashed over the hull again, drenching her hair and neck. She gasped.

"We're going to sink!" Jennifer screamed.

"No, we're not, Jen." Megan forced her voice to be calm. "It's just water. People have crossed the Atlantic Ocean in kayaks. We won't sink. I promise, we won't sink."

She paddled hard. Although her arms and shoulders and back ached, and cried out for her to stop, she didn't rest. After all, it was her fault they were in this mess in the first place. It was her fault they had to get help for the baby. When she dipped her paddle into the waves, she lashed out at them. "Take that and that and that," she muttered to the heaving sea.

When she couldn't stand the pain in her arms any longer she stopped, but only for a brief moment to catch her breath. The boat's nose started lurching uncontrollably in the sea. It was at the mercy of the waves, so she had to attack the water again.

Eventually, a bulky shadow appeared to her left. As they approached it, the outline of an island slowly emerged out of the mist. Trees and bushes grew down to the rocky shore.

"That must be Goose Island. I'm sure we can find the shortcut now."

The sea seemed calmer here in the lee of the island. She breathed a sigh of relief. Land!

ELEVEN

They stopped paddling for a moment and stared at Goose Island. They seemed to be drifting toward a narrow gap between it and their own Eagle Island.

"It feels like the current is pulling us the right way. What luck!" said Megan. "We'll just paddle through that gap. The tide looks high enough to let us through. Then it's just a short paddle around the top of the island to Dale Point where Dad is. I saw it on his chart. Think we can do it?"

"Okay," nodded Jennifer. She sounded exhausted.

Megan noticed a dark form on the approaching shore of their island. It was moving. "Looks like a dog on the beach ahead. I didn't know there were any stray dogs around here, did you?"

Jennifer shook her head and stared at the animal.

As they paddled closer Megan saw that it was not

a furry brown dog at all. It was a furry brown bear! It rose up on its hind legs and sniffed the air. It must have caught their scent because it scrambled down the beach over the rocks and splashed into the water, and started swimming toward them!

"A bear!" yelled Jennifer. "Paddle! Paddle harder, Meg! We've got to get away!" Her voice rose to a shriek.

"It's just a cub," Megan grunted to herself. It was no bigger than a large dog. It's true that cubs had sharp claws that could claw out your eyes, but they could outpaddle it. No prob.

Megan dug her paddle into the surf and pulled back hard. She tried to steer the boat away, but the cub was gaining on them.

"Turn it! Turn the boat away!" Jennifer yelled back at her.

"I'm trying to. But the current's got us. It's pulling us forward." Megan pressed her foot down hard on the left steering pedal.

"Meg! Watch out!" screamed Jennifer. "Watch out! There's another bear! On the other side!"

Out of the corner of her eye, Megan saw a dark movement on the opposite shore. She turned and stared.

Another bear! A huge one! It splashed into the water on their left and headed straight for them!

Megan froze in horror. Her heart leapt to her throat. She shook herself and gripped her paddle, pulling backward with all her might.

"Back paddle, Jen!" she yelled. "We've got to go back!"

The big bear roared at them, its mouth dripping with foaming water. The air was filled with its fury.

"Must be the cub's mother!" Megan yelled. "We're between her and her cub. We've got to get out of here! We've got to paddle backward!"

Jennifer crouched down in the boat and pulled her jacket over her head.

"Jennifer! Sit up! You've got to help! Paddle! We've got to work against this current. It's taking us straight toward that bear!"

But Jennifer was screaming with terror now. She cowered even lower into the boat. She'd be no help. Megan had to do this herself. She tried to force the boat backward by back paddling, but the current was far too strong. The boat was drifting swiftly into the path of the mother bear!

The bear plowed through the water, snarling and bellowing, pushing a furious surge of water forward.

Megan whirled her paddle around and bashed the boat's hull near Jennifer's cockpit. "Jennifer!" she screamed. "You've got to help!"

The bear lashed out in the direction of the boat's bow, its sharp claws glistening.

Jennifer shrieked and ducked even lower into the boat.

Megan shrieked too. She bashed the boat's hull again with all her might. "You get away from my sister!" she screamed. "You get away! Leave us alone!" She whacked the water with her paddle.

The bear growled again, its huge mouth widened

to reveal dripping fangs.

"I said get away," Megan screamed. "You get away from us! Get away! Get away!"

The boat rocked violently from side to side. Megan threw her weight to the right. Then she lurched left. She struggled desperately to keep the boat upright, so it wouldn't capsize and throw them into the water, into the bear's clutches.

The bear rose up again, roaring at them.

It was so close she could smell its fishy breath. She gripped the paddle in both hands and raised it high, then brought it down, walloping the water again.

The bear bellowed. The air vibrated.

Megan struck the water again, swinging the paddle over her head with both hands.

The bear reeled away.

Megan dug into the foaming surf with all her strength and paddled forward. Escape! They had to escape!

"You've got to paddle!" she yelled at Jennifer.

But Jennifer still cowered, paralyzed with fear.

Megan dug into the water again and pulled back, her arms straining. They were no longer fighting the current. The boat slipped forward.

The bear rose up from the water like a submarine rising from the deep and lunged toward them.

Megan gasped and yanked back on the paddle so hard she could feel all the muscles in her shoulders strain. With all her might, she dragged the boat out of the bear's path and paddled into the current, fast and strong and hard, until her breath tore at her throat, until her shoulders and arms were numb, until her heart threatened to leap from her chest. Then she paddled some more. She stared ahead, past Jennifer who was paddling hard now too. The current had caught them and was propelling them forward, toward the gap between the two islands. Megan concentrated on each swell as it raised the boat. Her breath came in short, sharp gasps. The pulse in her neck throbbed.

She paddled and paddled until she heard Jennifer whoop, "We did it, Meg! We did it! We got away from that old mama bear! We did! We did it!"

Megan slowed her paddling and turned back to see that the bear was way off in the distance.

Jennifer glanced over her shoulder. She was grinning from ear to ear.

"How about that?" Megan said, grinning back at her. "What a terrific team we are! The best paddling sisters in the west!"

The current flushed them through the narrow passage between the two islands and the water was so shallow they could see the rocky bottom slip by, just below the boat.

Now all they had to do was paddle up to the north end of the island. After what they had been through, that was going to be, as their father would say, "a piece of cake."

They followed the island's steep cliffs on their right until they came to a reef and some rocks protruding from the water. Megan turned the kayak out into deeper water and continued paddling.

"There's a boat!" shouted Jennifer as they rounded a steep rock. "Look!"

A small blue motorboat blasted out of a shallow bay. It wasn't *The Irish Lass*.

"And don't you ever come back!" Megan heard someone yelling from shore. It was their father! He was shaking a fist at the departing boaters. In his other hand he held his axe.

"You're crazy, man!" someone yelled from the speedboat. "Crazy!" The boat roared past their kayak, rocking it with its wake.

Megan struggled to keep the kayak from flipping over, leaning this way and that. Before the wake died and the seas calmed, she shouted, "Dad! Over here!"

Jennifer yelled too. "Dad! Dad!"

"Megan! Jennifer! My God!" He dropped his axe and ran toward them on shore. "Where did you two come from? How on earth …?"

"It's Joey!" Megan yelled. She paddled the boat within a few metres of him.

He splashed through the water until he could grab the boat's nose. "What is it?" His hair and beard were sticking out all over the place.

"Joey," Megan said again. "He's hurt. He hit his head. Needs stitches, a doctor."

Her father gasped and grabbed the boat's hull tighter. "No!" He shook his head. "Not the baby. Not my Joey." His eyes were frantic. "What is it? How did it happen?"

"It's a long story. We've got to get back to the cabin, so we can take him to the hospital."

"Right. Come on. Let's go."

He hurriedly dragged the kayak into shallower water and held it while the girls scrambled out.

They pulled it up onto the beach then frantically splashed through the water to his motorboat.

"We'll pick them up," Megan's father was panting, dragging up the anchor. "Take him to the emergency clinic in town."

Megan lifted Jennifer up over the hull and scrambled in after her just as her father started the motor and took off, a plume of spray erupting behind them.

The trip that had taken what felt like hours by kayak, took only minutes with their father's boat cruising at full throttle. He slowed down only to pick his way through the narrow channel between the islands. Megan scanned the beaches. The bears were long gone.

Bridget was waiting for them at their dock, huddled under the poncho, with the baby cradled in her arms. Her face was so pale that her faint freckles stood out on her cheeks and nose like flecks of pepper on a boiled egg. Deep circles bruised her eyes.

"How is he?" asked Megan's father, scrambling onto the dock.

"I've been out of my mind with worry. He seems to be sleeping now, but he's still bleeding."

Megan's father gently lifted the cloth from the baby's head. The jagged gash was still oozing blood.

"Oh, God!" He bit his lip and hugged Bridget's shoulders. "He's lost so much blood! Looks serious. We have to get him to the clinic right away."

Megan shut her stinging eyes. It's all my fault. If only I had been more careful. If only I hadn't tried to lift him. If only, if only … But she didn't have time to feel sorry for herself.

In minutes they were bundled into the boat and speeding out of the bay, heading toward Vancouver Island.

Bridget cradled the baby in her arms, rocking him back and forth, crooning to him.

Megan swallowed and shook her head. She thought about how much Bridget must love Joey, how worried she must be. Any mother would feel that way about her child. Even the mother bear had fought ferociously to protect her cub. She thought about how her own mother must be feeling right now, about her and Jennifer. She was probably out of her head with worry.

They had been missing for more than two days now and they had still not contacted her — no phone message, nothing, just the short note Megan had left on her pillow.

Jennifer was sitting beside her, hunched against the cold wind. "It's okay, little guys," she whispered to her turtles. "Don't be afraid." She held the turtle box under her coat and looked up at Megan, fear clouding her grey eyes. "Where are we going now?"

"Back to town, I think. You know the place, where we first boarded Dad's boat, where the taxi dropped us off?"

"I'm scared, Meg. I want to go home now and see Mommy," she sniffed.

"I know, Jen. I know." Megan put her arm around her and huddled closer to shelter her from the wind. She put her other hand into her coat pocket and touched the eagle carving. Her fingers explored the bird's hooked beak, its smooth back, its folded wings.

The trip back to town seemed much shorter than when they had first come to Eagle Island. The boat screamed across the wide channel and didn't slow down until they were in view of the dock.

Their father quickly moored the boat, leapt out and dashed up the dock to the road to flag down a passing car. Meanwhile, Megan climbed out onto the dock and grabbed the line to hold the boat close to the edge. Her father soon raced back and tied it up. "I found someone who will take us to the emergency clinic in town. It's not far."

They all bundled into the car, Bridget and the baby in front and the girls and their father in the back. They didn't even have time to buckle their seat-belts before the driver sped away. He was a young fellow who expertly manoeuvered the car up the steep hills and around the corner to the clinic. He stopped at the front door and Bridget scrambled out with the baby and disappeared inside.

"Thanks very much," said Megan's father to the young driver.

"Don't mention it. I hope your baby will be okay."

"Here's the waiting room," said Megan's father, showing the girls into a small room beside the entrance. "You two can wait in here. You'll be okay?"

"Joey's going to be all right, isn't he?" asked Jennifer.

Her father nodded, but when he looked at Megan, his eyes were filled with despair. He rushed away.

Megan took a deep breath, sat down and looked around the waiting room. It smelled of antiseptic. She automatically counted the chairs. There were six of them. Six shiny, brown plastic chairs and a low table with a pile of old magazines. She and Jennifer were the only ones there.

Jennifer sat on the edge of one of the chairs and rocked her turtles, humming tunelessly. She stopped and, with a tremor in her voice, said, "When do you think we'll be going home? I really miss Mommy. I want to see her now."

Megan nodded. "I know what you mean, Jen." She flipped through the magazines. No comics. She took out her eagle carving and her knife and started working. She whittled away, working on the long folded wings, carving them until they were feathered and smooth.

After a long while their father and a young woman dressed in a nurse's smock came into the waiting room. She got him a glass of water from a water cooler. "Now, Mr. Arnold," she said. "Calm down and drink this. You are no help to us getting so worked up."

He drank the water and sat down on one of the plastic chairs, nodding.

When the nurse left, Megan asked, "How's Joey? Has the bleeding stopped?"

Her father shrugged and bit his lip, blinking hard. He got up and paced around the waiting room. Then, abruptly, he sat back down. He put his hands up to his face and rocked back and forth. "He's got to be all right. He's just got to!" he moaned.

Megan nodded.

"I must have been crazy," he went on. "What was I thinking? Sooner or later there was bound to be an emergency. It could have been Bridget, or one of you. We always needs help. I see that now. First thing tomorrow, we're getting a cell phone. No messing around."

After a while the nurse returned.

"Mr. Arnold. Your son … You can come in now."

They all sprinted to the examining room. Bridget was sitting, cradling the baby in her arms. A long tube was taped to his arm, and a fresh bandage covered his forehead. Bridget smiled at them. "Our Joey is going to be fine. Just fine. Eleven stitches, he had."

The doctor was removing her rubber gloves. "Looks like there's no concussion, but he's lost a lot of blood for such a little fellow. Give him a few days and he'll be right as rain. We'll have to keep him here overnight though, just to be on the safe side."

Megan's father hugged Bridget gently, stroking her hair. He took out a large hanky and dabbed his eyes.

"Thank you, doctor," he said gruffly. "Thank you so much."

"It's a good thing you got him here when you did," said the doctor. "Now, Bridget, why don't you come with me. Maybe one of the girls could hold her brother for a minute while I show you to the restroom."

"I'll hold him," said Megan, for once stepping forward before Jennifer. She sat in an armchair and held out her arms.

Bridget gently placed Joey into her arms and smiled at her. "Thank you, Meg," she said, touching her cheek gently. She and Megan's father followed the doctor out of the room.

Joey was bundled up in clean hospital blankets now. He smelled fresh and sweet. She rocked him gently back and forth, humming the only tune she could think of. " 'Found a peanut, found a peanut, found a peanut last night ...' " He was as soft and warm as a kitten. He stirred, stretching his legs and wrinkling his nose. Then he blinked his dark eyes and stared up at her.

She stared back at him and caught her breath. It was like looking into a mirror, into her own dark eyes — her *brother's* eyes! She hugged him gently.

He blew a bubble through small pursed lips and gurgled at her, waving his arms.

Jennifer leaned on the arm of the chair and made faces at him. "He's so cute, isn't he?"

Megan reached into her pocket for the eagle carving. When she held it out to his hand, his tiny fingers curled around it and he cooed at her. "He's brilliant," she smiled. For some reason, her eyes were stinging like crazy. "Our little brother's just brilliant."

When Bridget returned with their father, she gently gathered Joey out of Megan's arms. Her father suggested that they all go out for fish and chips to celebrate.

"Before we go, Dad," said Megan. "Could we use the phone here?"

"I suppose so. Why?"

She took a quick breath and looked right at him. "I want to call Mom," she told him firmly.

He didn't blow up as she expected. He just blinked at her and said, "Your mother?"

She nodded. "She'll be crazy with worry. It's really not fair. I have to call her and tell her where we are and that we're safe. And Jen and I want to go back home. It's where we belong, Dad."

He gnawed his lower lip and sighed. "If that's how you feel, Meg." He stared down at Joey, his shoulders slumped. "Maybe you're right."

"Of course Megan's right," said Bridget. "You can't keep the girls hidden away. Their mother will be frantic."

He nodded finally and said, "I'll show you where the phone is."

Megan followed him along the hallway to a public phone on a wall beside a window. The phone was shiny black and reminded her right away of her mother.

"Just press zero and ask for the operator. She'll connect you," her father smiled at her, the crinkles fanning from the corners of his eyes.

She took a deep breath and dialled.

"Mom? It's Megan. Jen and I are safe. And we want to come home now."

TWELVE

"When is she going to get here?" asked Jennifer for the fifth time. She was wiggling in her seat across from Megan.

Sunshine filtered through the tall evergreen trees that lined the edge of the parking lot. They were waiting at a table outside the restaurant in the motel where they'd spent the night with their father. Bridget had stayed overnight at the clinic with Joey.

Their father had already been to a meeting earlier that morning. "AA meets for coffee every weekday morning at the community centre," he had told them. "And this time I'm sticking with it. From now on, I'm off the bottle for good." But he shifted restlessly beside Megan, twisting his coffee stir stick with trembling fingers. He flicked the stick away and spun his felt hat around and around on his knee.

"There she is!" squealed Jennifer. "There's Mom!"

Before the red Celica had turned into the parking lot beside the restaurant, Jennifer had rushed down the steps to the car. Megan followed her.

Their mother pulled to a halt and swung open the car door. Jennifer leapt into her arms and burrowed into her coat.

Megan hesitated for an instant. She must be so furious with her.

Her mother's hair was uncombed and her pale face was free of makeup. She was wearing a rumpled pair of black pants and an old green coat. But when she opened her arms wide and smiled up at Megan, it was her usual warm smile where the side of her mouth curved upward.

Megan dove and buried her head in her mother's soft powdery smell and strong shoulders.

"Oh, I'm so glad to see you," her mother murmured. "How I missed you two! I was so worried. Do you know how worried I was?"

"Mom, mom, mommy." Jennifer's mutters were muffled by their mother's coat. "You're here! You're finally here!"

"When you two didn't show up at the mall, I didn't know what could have happened to you. I thought you'd been delayed at the library so I called, but no one had seen you. After waiting for an hour or so, I went back home, but you weren't there either. That's when I found the note on your pillow, Meg. Was I ever mad! All my plans for our weekend down the drain."

"Sorry, Mom," said Megan. Before she had a chance to explain, her mother turned angrily to her father.

"How could you do such a thing, Joseph?" she demanded, her voice shrill. "Just take the girls away like that without telling me. And after we'd talked about it and everything. I told you we had other plans for the weekend. Didn't you think I'd be worried?"

He shook his head. "I just wanted to see them. I *had* to see them. It had been such a long time. They are my daughters too, don't forget."

"But to steal them away like that! What could you have been thinking? I called your apartment and you didn't even have your answering machine on."

"I don't spend much time there these days." He fidgeted with his hat, turning it around and around in his hands. "I know that I shouldn't have taken the girls away without your consent, but I really wanted to see them. And when I called last week and you said I couldn't, well ... I really miss them a lot."

"I don't care how much you miss them. You can't just show up and take them away like this. You have to ask me and I have to agree. And it's only fair that you give me enough notice. If it hadn't been for that note Megan left, I'd have thought they had been kidnapped or something. I would have called the police right away and they would have been out searching for you. Actually, last night just before Megan phoned, I was about to call them anyway."

"I want to see the girls more often, Patricia. How about a weekend early next month, before the weather gets too cold? I could come down and pick them up after school on a Friday?"

Megan's mother shook her head. "I'll have to think about that. Imagine taking the girls away to an island, without even a change of clothes. You must be crazy! I don't know if I can ever trust you again, or if they can, for that matter." She stared at him, her thin eyebrows raised angrily. "I'm not sure you could even look after them properly for a day, much less for a whole weekend."

"We don't need looking after, Mom," said Megan. "After all, I am twelve now."

"And there's Bridget to take care of us," said Jennifer.

"Bridget?"

"Yes. Joey's mother," said Jennifer.

"Oh," their mother nodded. "Oh, I see. Joey, is it?"

"He's our new brother and he's so cute. Only he fell and got hurt so he had to get all stitched up at the clinic. But he'll be better soon. Right, Meg?"

Megan nodded. All at once, she felt exhausted. Although it was only eleven o'clock in the morning, it already felt as if it had been a very long day. "Let's go home, Mom. Can we leave now?"

Her mother looked as if she had a lot more to say to her father, but she sighed and nodded.

Her father reached over to hug Megan good-bye, but she slipped into the front seat of the car instead.

He blinked at her sadly and helped Jennifer into the back seat. "See you two soon, I hope," he said. His voice was gruff so he cleared his throat. "I'm off to get a cell phone so you'll be able to call me any time you want. Things will be a lot better next time. You'll see. I promise."

Megan wasn't sure that there would be a next time. She knew all about his promises. Like her mother said, could she ever really trust him?

As they left the parking lot, she watched him out the rear window. He stood there looking forlorn, his old felt hat raised in farewell.

She squinted at the sun shining through the windshield. They were heading south down the Island Highway. A green blur of trees and an occasional glimpse of the ocean whizzed by. Jennifer dozed in the back seat.

Megan was hot, so she pulled off her sweatshirt. As she did so, she got a whiff of her smelly armpits. She saw her mother's nose wrinkle.

"So I guess your father's new place doesn't have a shower?"

"No. He hasn't hooked it up yet." Megan tried to keep her arms close to her sides to avoid the smell.

"Do you know how worried I was when I found your note?" asked her mother. "I don't understand how you could sneak off with him like that without even telling me."

"I'm really sorry, Mom. It's just that when you said we couldn't visit him, I got so mad. It just wasn't fair to him or to us. It's been almost a year since we'd last seen him. So when he phoned back and asked me to meet him and to bring along Jen, I really, really wanted to see him."

"I guess I can understand why you want to spend time with him, but I don't know if that's such a good idea right now." Her mother kept her eyes on the winding road. "For one thing, it looks to me like he's still drinking and you know the way alcohol affects him. It seems to make him lose all sense of reality. I wouldn't trust his judgment right now."

"He said he's giving up the bottle and he's joined AA again. He already went to a meeting this morning."

Megan's mother nodded. "That's a start, I guess, but we'll have to wait and see if he can stick with it this time before there'll be any more visits."

"But he *is* my father. Besides, he's the only one who ever really listens to me. He makes me feel, well, important. Most of the time anyway. And it's like he *wants* to spend time with us. It's not just a duty for him, which is a lot more than I can say for you."

"What do you mean? We do things together, don't we? Like that musical we were supposed to have gone to this weekend. You know how much I had to pay for those tickets? And we go shopping. What about those expensive designer jeans I buy you all the time?"

Megan shook her head. "That's not what I mean. I mean just hanging out and talking. You don't have to spend a whole lot of money. You don't even watch TV with us anymore. You're always too busy. Even at dinner time you're usually on the phone, talking to your clients."

Her mother sighed. "I guess that's true. I have been

busy lately. But it's not easy being a single parent these days. And hard work is the only way to get ahead. There's so much competition out there."

"And that's another thing. Do you have to practise on our place all the time? Why can't we have just an ordinary house like my friends have?"

"So you don't like the new black kitchen?"

"I hate it! It's like living in a museum of modern art or something."

Her mom snorted. "Maybe you're right, Meg," she said. "It is a bit austere. I've been thinking of changing it to a retro theme. Retro is very popular these days. You know, turquoise and sunny yellow. More cheerful. The Seventies look."

"That's not the point, Mom. You're *still* not listening to me. When was the last time you and Jen and I went to the beach? Not once during the whole summer."

"You're right. I know, you're right. I had time to really think about us this weekend. I realized that I've been so buried in my work that I've been neglecting you two. All I can say is that I'll try harder. Maybe I'll take next weekend off and spend the whole time with you two."

"And what about us visiting Dad?"

"As I said, we'll have to see about that. If he can stay away from drinking, there's no reason he can't have you over to visit sometimes, if you really want to go. Especially now that there's another adult in the picture."

Megan nodded. She folded the sweatshirt her father had given her and crossed her arms over it. She leaned her head on the backrest and sighed.

Her mother reached over and patted her hand. "You okay, Meg?"

"Yeah," she nodded and squeezed her mother's fingers. "I'm all right now."

ACKNOWLEDGMENTS

I would like to thank my fellow writers, especially Sonia Craddock and James Heneghan for their insightful comments and enthusiasm after reading early drafts of this novel.

Also, I would like to thank my editor, Joy Gugeler, for her unfailing encouragement and vision of the novel and her perseverance in editing it.

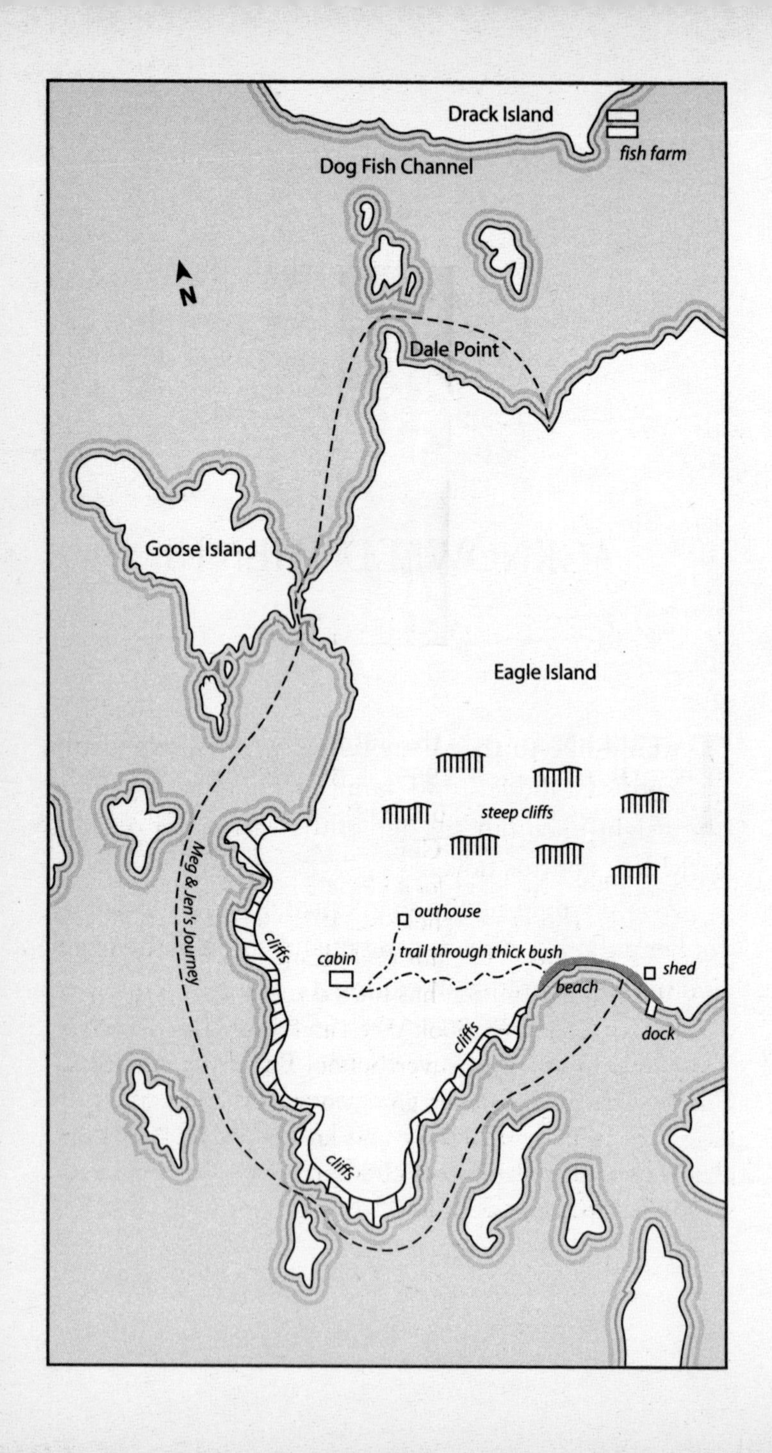
Drack Island
fish farm
Dog Fish Channel
N
Dale Point
Goose Island
Eagle Island
steep cliffs
Meg & Jen's Journey
cliffs
outhouse
cabin
trail through thick bush
shed
beach
dock
cliffs
cliffs

Norma Charles is the author of *Sophie Sea to Sea* (Beach Holme, 1999), a BC 2000 Award Winner, *Runaway* (Coteau, 1999), *Dolphin Alert* (Nelson, 1998), *Darlene's Shadow* (General, 1991), *April Fool Heroes* (Nelson, 1989), *No Place for a Horse* (Overlea House, 1988) and *Amanda Grows Up* (Scholastic, 1978). Her first children's book, *See You Later, Alligator* (Scholastic, 1976, 1991) sold over 100,000 copies. She has toured widely to schools and libraries for Children's Book Week and worked as a teacher librarian with the Vancouver School Board for ten years. Charles lives in Vancouver, gives workshops and writes full time. She is an avid kayaker and knows the Gulf Islands almost as well as she knows children; she is the mother of six and has four grandchildren.

More Raincoast YA Fiction:

***Wishing Star Summer* by Beryl Young**
1-55192-450-1 $9.95 $6.95 US
Jillian, a lonely eleven year old, has struck upon an ingenious solution to her friendless existence in grade six: Tanya, a Belarus girl exposed to Chernobyl radiation, will stay with her family on a summer exchange. But when language barriers, poor health and culture shock strain the relationship Jillian must learn to be a friend in order to have one.

***Cat's Eye Corner* by Terry Griggs**
1-55192-350-5 $9.95 $6.95 US
When Olivier visits his grandfather, retired to Cat's Eye Corner with a reported witch, he finds himself on a strange scavenger hunt in the Dark Wood. Soon he is knee-deep in adventures with the So-So Gang, a talking pen, a girl named Linnett who controls the wind and mischievous word fairies called Inklings.

***Dead Reckoning* by Julie Burtinshaw**
1-55192-342-4 $9.95 $6.95 US
Fourteen-year-old James boards the steamship *Valencia* in San Francisco's harbour in 1906 unprepared for the violent storm that forces the crew to rely on dead reckoning. When the vessel runs aground in seas too rocky for rescue, James and his friend Alex board the last lifeboat …

***Raven's Flight* by Diane Silvey**
1-55192-344-0 $9.95 $6.95 US
In Silvey's fourth book, fifteen-year-old Raven searches for her missing sister, Marcie, reportedly "working" on Vancouver's lower east side. But when Raven learns that Marcie is wanted by a kidnapping ring abducting children to be smuggled across the Pacific, Raven must put together clues from Marcie's diary before it's too late.